DEAD AND BACK AGAIN #1

SPECTER INSPECTOR

C. RAE D'ARC

Cover design by 100 Covers

ISBN: 978-1-961733-09-1 (paperback)

Published by Bursting Box Publishing

www.craedarc.com
www.facebook.com/c.rae.darc
www.instagram.com/craedarc

Praise for the Haunted Romance Trilogy

Don't Date the Haunted

"Certain to have the reader laughing out loud."
– *Readers' Favorite*

"Sitting on my 'Best Books I've Ever Read' shelf."
– *Gee Liz Reads*

Don't Marry the Cursed

"Rating: 10/10 I can't wait for the next one!"
– *Leyendo.Lina (Bookstagrammer)*

"Don't Pass Up This Series."
– *Jim Doran, author of Kingdom series*

Don't Dance with Death

"Am I allowed to call this a perfect trilogy?"
– *Valerie Evans, author of Wolves of Worsham series*

"Exciting and engaging from the very beginning."
– *Libromancy Podcast*

Books by C. Rae D'Arc

HAUNTED ROMANCE
Don't Date the Haunted
Don't Marry the Cursed
Don't Dance with Death

* * *

Oz's Haunting Survival Book
From Horror with Love

DEAD AND BACK AGAIN
Specter Inspector

DREAMING PRINCESSES
Dreaming Beauty
Fairest and the Frog
Little Red and the Lumpy Bed

To the "oddballs" and "freaks."
Stay weird.

"I can assure you," said I,
"that it will take a very tangible ghost to frighten me."
- *The Red Room*, by HG Wells

World of Novel

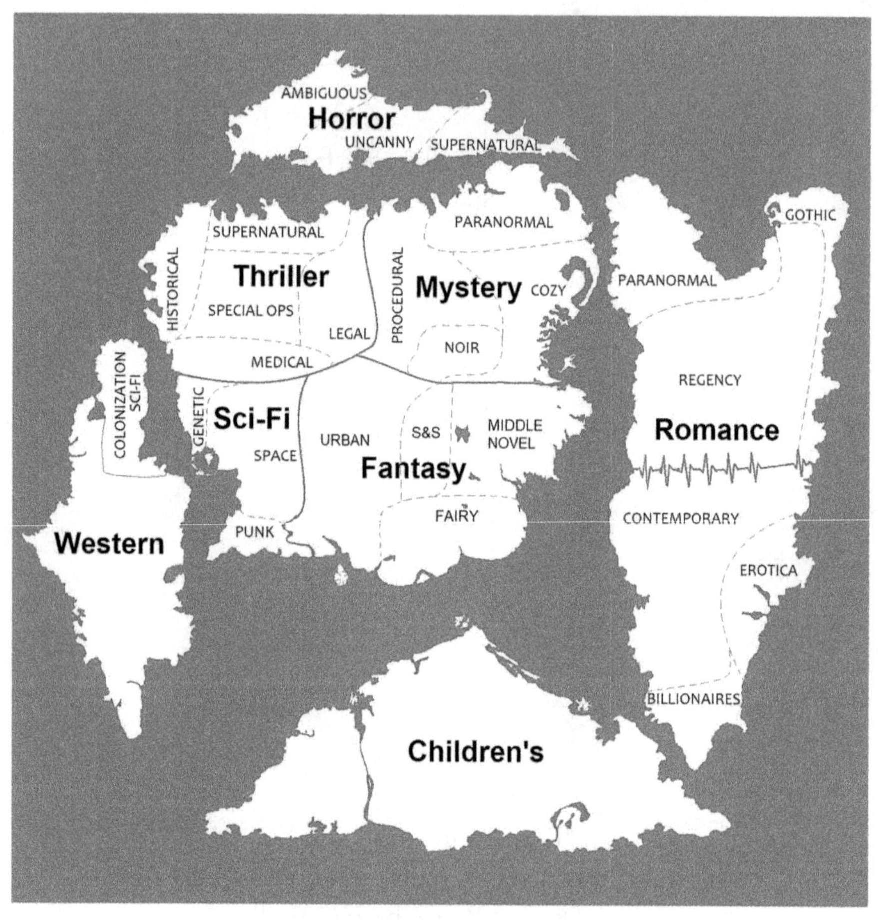

DEAD AND BACK AGAIN #1

SPECTER INSPECTOR

CHAPTER 1

Verily, these detectives of Mystery, no matter their
competence, do prove among the most obstinate folk,
unwilling to abandon a mystery while unsolved.
(#1 characteristic: determination. Check.)

- *Lemuel Gulliver's Travel Guide,
Vol. 4: Mystery*
(with notes by Aeron)

I hope you like ghost stories. Then, I hope you're comfortable, reclined in your favorite chair or laying down with blankets all around you. It seems like there's never enough time to read, especially when life gets confusing and all you want to do is escape to another life in another world.

So, let me welcome you to my life in the world of Novel and explain the reason I'm talking directly to you like this. The story I'm about to tell began six days ago, in Noir, Mystery. More specifically, in the smoky city of Shigaqua, where the line blurs most between friends and foes, mentors and monsters, and victims and villains.

The only part of the States of Mystery that makes sense is its dense population of law enforcers and private investigators—

which I hoped to join. It makes as much sense as magic in Fantasy, horses in Western, spaceships in Sci-Fi, monsters in Horror, kids in Children's, and lovers in Romance.

Sure, the world of Novel is always in flux. Children's is outright chaos, and Western is untamably wild. Romance finally cracked down on their vampire problem, but lately, Fantasy fairies have found ways to keep their powers there. Mystery, however, is and always has been the land of truth seekers.

I only fit in because I can find the answers. Talking to the dead in my sleep has that kind of advantage.

So, let me take you back, six days before I woke in a cold sweat with a vivid memory of a dead man screaming in my face, roaring for justice at the price of everything I'd hoped to achieve.

I fidgeted with the latch of my leather bracelet while sitting in the hallway outside the head investigator's office of Silent Sleuth Services, Shigaqua's leading private investigations agency. Three more occupied chairs lined up beside me, with six vacant. I'd made it this far in the job application process, but ten of us still remained.

Clasping and unclasping my leather bracelet kept me from fidgeting with my other articles of clothing, which included a tweed pale blue suit vest over a white long-sleeve shirt, and gray dress-slacks over leather combat boots. Women said they liked the light colors contrasting with my dark brown hair, blue-green eyes, and opposite-of-ghostly complexion.

A man in his mid-forties wearing a corduroy suit stepped from the office, chewing on his lip. I took a small comfort in the thought that even someone of his age could be nervous about a job interview. Except that also meant that someone with his life experiences was still nervous about getting this job.

The secretary who'd greeted each of us didn't invite the next applicant immediately. I held my breath, hoping it would be me. Another applicant feigned tranquility as he read the day's *Shigaqua Times*, but his foot bounced nervously. Not that I could judge his nerves. I sat on my foldable metal chair and clasp-unclasp-clasp-unclasped. Despite my ability to literally solve crimes in my sleep, I had to climb the corporate ladder like everyone else to become a private investigator.

I held my breath again as the secretary released a plume of her cheap cigarette smoke, adding to the haze that yellowed the ceiling. Welcome to Noir. Curses, I missed the health codes of Procedural.

Every state in Mystery had its own requirements to become a PI. In Cozy, you could be no more than a nosy busybody. I pitied the legitimate cops in that state. On the other hand, in Procedural, I needed to be older with twenty years of police service. My specific talents best fit in Paranormal, but I preferred to be a big fish in a little pool. So, out of all the states to become a private investigator, I wanted to work in Noir. Plus, I'd get to wear a trench coat.

A small light blinked on the secretary's desk, and she looked up. She was a pretty little damsel in her knee-length pencil skirt and matching gray suit top. Her blouse featured a black bow at her collar that was bigger than her chest. She breathed out another cough-inducing cloud before speaking.

"Aeron Spade?" she stated more than questioned, but Mystery accents tended to make everything sound like questions.

"Yes, ma'am!" I stood at attention, then mentally slapped myself. Nothing painted me as foreign fresh meat like treating Mystery officials as the military.

The secretary raised an eyebrow but gestured for me to enter the office. "Head Investigator Baldi is ready for you."

I gulped heavily and walked up. There was a window from the hallway into the office, but it was blocked with blinds. Only in Mystery. Why bother installing windows that only reveal more indoors and then cover them with shades? Seemed unnecessary and counter-productive to me.

Entering the office, I subtly analyzed the work space of my prospective employer. After years of university classes and training on perception, it was difficult to miss Baldi's plaques of recognition, displayed as they were on the right wall with intricate frames. The left wall was occupied with a floor-to-ceiling bookshelf, stacked evenly with law books and Case histories. A tall wall-clock chimed the evening's eighth hour, and a caged fan crackled from the top of a filing cabinet. Despite the over-worked fan, a posh cigarette scent filled the room. Smothered ashes hissed from a tray on the ornate mahogany desk. An older *Shigaqua Times* sat folded on the corner, headlining, "Police Nickname Shigaqua's Elusive Mobster as 'Sponsor.'" Facing me, a nameplate read, "Head of Investigations, PI Baldi." Did anyone dare to call him Baldi Head?

The man edged forward in a stiff leather armchair behind his massive desk. I sat on the other side and consciously restrained my fidgeting.

PI Baldi was a large man who filled his leather armchair with both width and height. I expected a man of his age to wear spectacles, but saw no evidence of even reading glasses on his desk. He had a full head of thick black hair—no. I could just pick out the lining of a cheap toupee between his side-part. How appropriate.

"Aeron Spade," the man slurred over my name as he read it from my resumé. Go figure, reading made him squint. He also spoke with a heavy Mysterious accent that made every comment sound like a question. Sometimes, I thought Mysteries took their elusiveness a little too far. Even their Exit signs ended with question marks. I listened carefully to decipher between hypotheticals and interview questions. "You recently graduated from Spyglass University, huh? Wha'ja think of Procedural?"

Of the many practice interview questions I'd reviewed, that wasn't one of them. I cleared my throat and answered simply, "It was…plain."

Honestly, I wanted to say "clean." While Procedural had carefully cultivated parks and stark white buildings made of reflective metals, it also had too much paperwork. Noir, on the other hand, was the very definition of smokey: in appearance, scent, and even in their official Case results. Light tans and grays themed their fashions with occasional flashes of rusty blues and reds. Fog crept through the streets whenever the sun looked the other way, and lots of people smoked like they knew life was too short to worry about long-term health problems.

Head Investigator Baldi scoffed a kind of chuckle and returned to my resumé. "Aeron Spade, I called up your references. How'djoo get 'em all to call you the 'Ace of Spades?' What if I call you Aeron Fromm of Margen, Fantasy?"

I gulped. "And now you know why I asked you not to pass pre-judgements on me from the background checks. Please know, I've cut myself off and have lived away from Fantasy for over five years now. I'm determined to make my own way."

"As if we can ignore your parentage? You know we're pros at doin' background checks, right?"

"Yes, sir. Please, I ask to be reviewed and interviewed as any other applicant."

He scoffed and shuffled my resumé back into order. "You're livin' under an alias. How'm I to know the rest of this ain't a bunch of bull? Even your age. You expect me to believe you're only twenty and already got a Masters in Law?"

"And a Minor in Criminal Justice." I pointed at my resumé where it was indicated. "I was provided an accelerated education, and I can multitask in my sleep."

The man stared at me as if still waiting for an explanation.

I sighed and met his eyes directly. "It's my ability. I wrote about it in my skills section. I enter the spirit realm in my sleep and use the time to research, review notes, or follow people unseen. I've also used my ability to communicate with deceased persons and solve Cases. I'd like to do so officially with a Permanent Employee Registration Card, sponsored by your agency."

"You have magic? From Fantasy? You know that bull only works in Paranormal, Mystery, right?"

"It isn't exactly magic," I explained. "The difference is a common misunderstanding. Magic is a learned trade that, yes, diminishes or mutates outside of Fantasy. Abilities, however, are inherited from birth and focus around a specific skill, but they can transfer between continents without alteration." Though the spirits in Mystery were more reasonable to work with than the wanna-be gods in Fantasy.

The man blinked and shook his head. "That's how you got these creds despite bein' underage? Listen, kid, your resumé is squeaky clean, and if you had the experience, I'd hire you on the double. But that's the rub, ya see? You ain't got experience, and Shigaqua's no place for a Cozy."

My mind panicked, and I considered it a great victory that I didn't jump up and shout, "What do you mean I don't have experience? Can't you see the whole experience section on my resumé?"

Instead, I fidgeted with my bracelet and calmly asked, "Please explain?"

"I gotta hand it to ya, kid, you've solved some 'Cases,' but they're small fry. You helped a family find lost treasure by trackin' down a stiff and gettin' directions? And you solved a murder by talking to the victim? Alright, that's swell, but how much elbow grease did you put into that? Where's your proof? You think you can just hit the hay and chat with dead guys like it's nothin', and that'll hold up in court? By sittin' in that seat, you're applyin' for the big leagues. We got big-time crime here, and it ain't no picnic. How'd I know you got the gumption to roll up your sleeves and work hard like the rest of us?"

I nodded and continued to nervously fidget. Those were just summaries of my Cases, so of course they sounded easy on paper. I ran into problems all the time with my spiritual visits. A major one was trying to remember what happened after I woke up.

I bit the inside of my cheek to keep it from giving excuses. Excuses would not show that I was tough enough for the job. Besides, Mr. Baldi hadn't rejected me yet. He'd asked me to prove myself. I swallowed, but continued to fix my stare.

"If I may be frank, sir, I can guarantee that I'll work harder with more unpaid hours than any other investigator in your agency. Not simply because I can work in my sleep, but because Shigaqua is the place I want to be. I even signed a year-lease for my house. Not only do I dream of working with Silent Sleuth Services because of its highly recommended reputation, but it's my only option. Your agency is the only one open to hiring Fantastics like me." Finding an agency open to hiring a newbie was scarce enough without their prejudices as Mystery "purists."

I hated revealing my hand like that, but hopefully he saw my royal flush and took a bet on me. Having studied Silent Sleuth Services before applying, I'd noticed another investigator from Fantasy in his ranks. Her listed years of experience meant she'd been hired under Baldi's predecessor, Head Investigator Harry, but surely he'd recognize the benefits of my abilities. Right?

"Try me," I said, hoping to sound more challenging than desperate. "Just one Case—any Case. I'll solve it and prove myself."

Head Investigator Baldi leaned back in his chair and eyed me as if I was a ten-thousand-piece puzzle that he wasn't sure whether or not to open. Clasp-unclasp-clasp-unclasp.

He nodded thoughtfully. "When getting ready for these interviews, we set aside a few Cases to test our rookies. Listen, how about I give you a chance?" He leaned forward again to leaf through a small pile of folders on his desk. "How'djoo like to solve a Case reserved for a rookie?"

"Really?" I started to reach for the file, but he pulled it back.

"Did I say I was finished?"

"No, sir."

"Right. Listen, kid, this is a Criminal Defense Investigation. The subject has his trial next Monday. One week from today. We've been hired by his lawyer, who wants admissible proof of his innocence. You know what that means, kid?"

"Audio recording, still photos, video, or confession," I said.

"Not just that. The facts gotta be presented in a tight, well-written report if ya wanna provide a strong legal representation. Take note of every method and tool you use, and I ain't talkin' about sleepin' pills. Can ya prove to me you didn't just snooze your way through school? If ya can do that, kid, you're in."

"No problem," I said, trying to feel as confident as I sounded.

"You really think you can solve this Case in seven days?"

"My future career is on the line," I said. "You can bet on it."

"One week. Good luck, kid." He stood and handed me the file. We shook hands on the deal and to say goodbye.

My stomach was all sorts of jitters as I left the room. I'd be hired! I'd work in the most prestigious private investigations agency in all of Noir's capital! I'd be the youngest and best investigator in town! All I needed to do was solve this Case in seven days.

My feet stopped cold. Seven days. Cases, Adventures, Romances, and other big events of Novel life usually occurred once—maybe twice—a year. Up to that point, I had maximized my opportunities by hunting for one Case every semester, finishing with my capstone only two weeks ago. How was I supposed to solve this Case in a week?

Passing the other interview contestants, I tried to hide my anxious mix of excitement and doubt. One week wasn't much time at all. I looked beyond the contestants to the office rooms of official private investigators. Desks cluttered with newspaper clippings, notepads, and typewriters. Only one week, and I'd be working there with all the thrills and resources of an official PI.

Except...I wouldn't have those resources for this Case. I frowned. Without access to the files, the badge of an official, and clearance, I was limited. It might have been impossible for any other rookie. Lucky for me, I had resources on the other side.

CHAPTER 2

The so-called 'heroic' detective oft resorts to resources
of questionable nature.
(Does that include you, Lemuel?)

- *Lemuel Gulliver's Travel Guide,*
Vol. 4: Mystery
(with notes by Aeron)

Shigaqua was a lake port city on the south-eastern side of Mystery, stuck between historical and contemporary eras. On one hand, it had telephones, but on the other, all phones had spiral cords and rotary dials. We had handguns, but the mobsters had Tommy guns. At least my car was faster than theirs.

I drove home with the fastest car available with Noir's technology: an LXK120 Panther. It was so named for its luxurious two seats of leather, dashboard Smith clocks, and six-cylinder engine that could go the outrageous speed of a hundred-twenty miles per hour. Even better, it reached sixty in ten seconds. I had the black roadster refitted with a convertible top to adjust for the Shigaqua rain and a dial radio for news reports and big band music. To complete my personalization, I had blue smoke painted where most sports cars painted flames.

If I was going to turn heads with my car and reputation, I might as well leave the right impression. I was smoke: half physical, half spirit, and impossible to pin down.

"Can you believe it?" I asked the empty seat beside me, assuming that one of my ghostly friends sat there. Probably Morse. He loved my car even more than I did. "I have my first official Case! Okay, it's not official in the sense that I'm an official, but it was given to me by an official, and it'll be the Case that makes me an official PI of Mystery! Finally! After all these years! Okay, yes, I'm only twenty, and most people are much older when they get to this stage, but—"

"*Aeron,*" a voice said so subtly that it was barely more than a thought in my mind. "*Keep your eyes on the road, would you?*" Yep, that was Morse.

"What? I can't be excited? Can't you be excited with me?"

Memories of lectures and lessons on driving defensively streamed through my mind.

"Oh, shush. You're no fun." I blasted my radio to drown his lectures, catching even more stares from pedestrians.

Most investigators tried to blend in and remain anonymous in the crowd for better sleuthing. With my reputation, I didn't have that luxury. Wherever I went, people cranked their necks, pointed, and whispered. They saw me for my young age, foreign status, and quick accomplishments.

Funny enough, having a loud reputation actually made it easier to disguise myself as a quiet passerby. No one expected to find someone like me under a ratty coat, unkempt beard, and fake nose.

I daydreamed of my ideal future as a private investigator with my own office in the city, slapping cuffs around Sponsor's wrists or another underworld headliner. I'd hire an innocently gorgeous secretary, and femme fatales would find their way to my office. They'd cry for help or kiss me until I agreed to take their Cases for a pittance. I enjoyed the thought of taking charity Cases between big jobs that would make front pages.

Until I was officially hired with an office or even a cubicle, that left me working from home. I drove to my rental house on 2210 Smoking Gun Lane in Shigaqua's north-western suburb of Rose Plaines. It was the closest rambler house I could find for a decent price and didn't have neighbors within spitting distance. The forty-minute commute was worth the privacy.

As a paranoid native of Horror, my mom stood against every part of my house, despite following her guidelines for no basements or attics and annual replacements of lights. Sure, my parents helped pay for my education, but my mom refused to pitch toward my bachelor pad. A second-floor apartment with several roommates would have been her preferred housing. As if I could convince anyone to board with me.

I quickly learned to live outside of dorms, apartments, condos, and even townhouses. Anyone who shared walls with my place of residence eventually asked me to be evicted. Roommates refused to share rooms with me. Those who tried, gave up within the first week then joined the crowds shouting, "Fantasy Freak."

This wasn't because I was a bad housekeeper or disruptive neighbor. I simply had a lot of dead visitors. Entering the spirit realm in my sleep turned my bedroom into a gathering place for ghosts. Naturally, that made it the number one most haunted room in whichever city I currently resided.

Neighbors gave my house a wide berth. Dog-walkers learned to stay away or suffer the consequences of mad barking, whining, or growling. Joggers crossed the street because the whispers began at the sidewalk. They were faint enough to brush away as "just the wind," though audible enough to cause doubts. When going up my walkway, the whispers became defined enough as voices, though they were too hushed to discern words. Mail carriers and delivery drivers brave enough to reach my door often screamed away after hearing disembodied voices ask, "*Who are you?*" "*What are you doing here?*" or (my personal favorite) "*Would you like some tea?*"

Sadly, this scared a lot of people. They didn't know what they were missing.

One positive was rarely worrying about housework because of the various influences of the spirits. Miss Fairlie, in particular, loved to garden and flourished my lawn with daisies. The front hedges changed shapes every few days. Morning glory climbed up the outside brick walls and through the window cracks until they framed around the inside ceilings. My living space was full of life despite the death that also resided inside.

When I approached, the voices were always different and generally spoke on the theme of "*Welcome,*" "*We await you on the other side,*" or again, "*Would you like some tea?*"

Tonight, as my car rumbled into my detached garage, a male voice whispered, "*We have been expecting you,*" and my house lights flickered on. Greetings from the old man in the corner. He loved to be the first one to welcome me. One of these days, I'd convince him to tell me his real name.

My car's dashboard registered the change of outside temperature from the driveway as Shigaqua's early summer nights boasted seventy-degrees. My new house had a thermometer… somewhere. Not that it mattered. The temperature dropped to my favorite familiar chill and humidity as I walked the twenty steps from my garage to my side entrance.

A paper flier wafted across my driveway. I dashed over to jump on it before the wind carried the litter away. Picking it up, I found an invitation to a neighborhood barbeque. For to-day. Checking my pocket-watch confirmed the event was already over.

Go figure. They "forgot" to invite me again because they were either too afraid to approach my haunted house or to call up the "not white" "Fantasy freak." I preferred the politically correct term for Fantasy natives as "Fantastics."

They could have asked the neighborhood teenagers. They loved daring each other to knock on my door.

Whatever. I didn't need living friends.

I tossed the paper into my outside trash bin and stepped inside.

I dropped my keys into a hollowed book safe and gave a longing look at the tan trench coat on the wall hanger. My little sister had given it to me as a graduation gift. One day soon, I hoped to wear it without feeling like an imposter.

Turning away, I was greeted with a scene that would have scared any normal person out of their wits. The curtains waved before closed windows, an empty rocking chair rolled back and forth, papers fluttered on my desk, the floorboards groaned with footprints in the dust, walls moaned, and the whispers of unembodied voices washed over one another. Faint images of people waved between reflections from my windows and mir-rors. The morning glory and ivy climbed an extra inch up the walls. My little house was crowded with the dead. Just how I liked it.

I specifically chose a house with an open layout and a bath-room in the middle. Then, I had removed all doors except the one into that center bathroom. Doors and walls meant nothing to ghosts, but that bathroom was off limits. A guy needed some privacy after all.

I waved to my unseen occupants and went directly to my refrigerator. Supernaturals, I was hungry. I'd been too nervous before my interview to eat dinner. With that over, I was famished.

My refrigerator consisted of the bare minimum basic food groups, a leftover Fantasy take-out meal, and a pitcher for filtered water. Mystery had some weird chemicals in its tap water. My freezer was stocked full of quick meals that required little to no cooking skills. I grabbed an apple and energy bar with unknown ingredients, then warmed a kettle for an unmarked packet of random tea flavors. Typical of Mystery.

I dearly missed the luxury and variety of foods from Fantasy but had to admit these city foods were mighty convenient. I took my little energy bar, cup of tea (apparently, it was cinnamon), and an apple to my desk, then set out the Case from Baldi.

Time to study.

I did a quick scan over the information, then did a second more-careful read through. The criminal defense investigation was labeled as the Quigley Case. Mr. William Quigley (a B-list actor) was accused of murdering his fifteen-year-old son, Richard Quigley, after dropping him off at the Regal Theater for his son's play rehearsal. The police did their jobs, pinning the father with witnesses of an argument between the victim and accused only moments before the death. But there weren't any visual witnesses when the boy had been pushed off the fifteen-foot catwalk and fell on his head. The murderer had escaped down the other end of the catwalk before anyone could spot them.

Though the file was fat with suspects, the notes and documents went from one dead end to the next. Mr. Quigley's excuse for an alibi stated that he "drove home alone" directly after their argument and before the fatal accident. Not good enough. Especially when a button from Mr. Quigley's jacket was found under the body, indicating an alleged struggle as

Richard tore the button free, then dropped it as he thrashed helplessly toward the stage. William Quigley had motive, means, and opportunity.

The timing of the Case confused me until I finished my initial read. Mr. Baldi had said the Case had been reserved for a rookie, though the incident in question had occurred nearly five months ago. Mr. Quigley was arrested and charged on the third day after his son's death. His wife must have believed in Mr. Quigley's innocence enough to push her lawyer into hiring Silent Sleuth Services to take a second look into the Case. Of course, the Quigleys and their lawyer wanted the investigators to find evidence to confirm his innocence, but that was the joy of being a third-party investigator. It was simply my job to find evidence—whether it freed or condemned the client—then let the attorney decide what to do with it.

By the looks of the extensive work on the Case and names on the reports, Silent Sleuth Services had already run the Case through three different investigators. The second set of investigators had declared it a waste of time, then the Case had been "reserved" on Baldi's desk as the third set was reassigned to a "more pertinent Case."

My anxiety-fueled adrenaline ended with a gradual, yet undeniable crash. My eyes drooped and head bobbed as I read and re-read the reports without comprehension.

I didn't want to fall asleep at my desk…again. With my last bit of energy, I wandered to my bathroom to prepare for bed.

Teeth brushed and dressed in long pajamas, I placed a notepad and pen on my nightstand, then climbed under the covers. The sheets were stiff and smelled a little too much like my sweat, but it was too late for laundry. The most annoying part about having the most haunted bachelor home was that I had to do all the cleaning myself.

Whatever. I had work to do, and that meant I needed to sleep. Punching my pillow into shape, I focused on relaxing my muscles and breathing slowly.

Two hours after falling asleep, I drifted from my body to float in the air. I was translucent and incorporeal, without gravity. As a spirit, I could glide through walls and objects of the mortal realm. Other spirits could create a sense of touch, though we always blew through each other with only a cold tingling or the mere memory of touch. That was the most frustrating part about being a spirit. I couldn't hug my best friends.

Speaking of which, some of the world's most renowned detectives floated at the foot of my bed.

"Ah, welcome back, Haunted Fromm," Sherlock Holmes said. I winced as he used my Fantasy names, but there were no secrets from the dead. "Might I suggest that you endeavor to rid yourself of your fidgeting? Your nervous habits reveal too much about your past and indicate an unstable mind. This trait is particularly detrimental in the field you aspire to enter."

"Come on, I didn't butcher it," I said. "I got the job! No celebration?"

Auguste Dupin said, "I must remind you that you have not yet been engaged for the task. Did your mother not popularize the phrase, 'Don't celebrate too early?'"

I shrugged. "Meh, he gave me a Case. The only thing I'm missing is a tax ID."

"And a badge," Hercule Poirot said.

"And the law enforcement resources," Detective Inspector Lestrade added.

"Details," I said with another shrug. "I have you guys! You all solved Cases without an agency and population censuses. So can I." I hoped to appear more confident than I felt. Sure, there was always somebody somewhere who had the answers I needed, but it usually required some research with the university resources to determine which spirit to look up.

"We had little concerning agencies," Holmes said, "but we had partners and connections."

I gestured my arms wide to them. "And what are you guys? Are you not my connections?"

Dupin sighed. "Fromm, it is imperative that you establish connections with the living."

"I suggest you begin with the vagrants," Holmes said.

"No, mate," Lestrade said firmly. "Start with your colleagues. It's the groundwork for any smooth investigation. Make new mates wherever you can and build trust with them."

"The vagrants," Holmes affirmed. "I rely on them to provide me with pertinent information, and in turn, they rely on me to compensate them for their efforts."

"May I suggest that you undertake a voyage?" Poirot said. "Not only is it enlightening and entertaining, but it affords you the opportunity to expand your sphere of influence and network across the globe."

I raised an eyebrow at him. "These are my travels. I'm not a native to Mystery." As such, Lemuel Gulliver (Fantasy's "God of Travels") had me strenuously memorize his traveling tips while sleeping to create a small book before I left Fantasy.

Poirot frowned. "Alors, where are all your nouveaux amis and connaissances?"

Without an answer, my hand instinctively went to fidget with my bracelet.

"Ah!" Holmes pointed. "No more fidgeting!"

"You guys are relentless. I bet Watson would be happy for me."

Unfortunately for me, Watson had married and had kids. While Sherlock's spirit was linked to the city of Shigaqua, Watson had linked to his descendants to fawn over and supervise in death.

They could move on to the Unknown Beyond any time they wanted, but some spirits chose to linger by linking themselves to certain people, places, or even things. Fantasy spirits were particularly fond of linking themselves to ideas, becoming gods of love, conquest, or the smell of berry pies. Poirot had linked to the idea of curiosity. He once described his link as a pull toward people who desired to learn and experience new things. As such, he often spent his time on the city's university campus, but made time for my nightly reports.

They often chose their links based on their supernatural gifts. While some spirits could travel with a blink like Poirot or Gulliver, to process information at lightning speeds like Lestrade, or even to appear to the living as a disguised helper like Sherlock, my gift was simply to return to the living every morning. Not that I was complaining.

My spiritual teachers were impossible to please, but I still considered them my friends.

"Alright," I said with an unnecessary exhale. "Let's see what we have to work with."

Lestrade waved his hand, and a small gust of air blew the file of papers on my desk. The file was fat with suspects between the victim's family and "friends" which included the playhouse's entire cast and crew. I began to read through them one by one while Lestrade directed me to specific pieces of interest. I didn't bother memorizing the exact wording as I did when studying for tests, but carefully reading over the information several times usually helped me to remember the concepts after waking. I made mental notes on each suspect regarding the three keys to solving any murder: motive, means, and opportunity.

Since it occurred during a dress rehearsal, the entire cast and crew had been present. Several of the actresses had firm alibis in the dressing room. I'd suspect a pact-killing except two boys confessed to spying on the girls through a hole in the second dressing room, verifying all dressing room alibis.

Director Stephens' alibi was that he was alone in the lobby bathroom, but the security cameras caught him walking through the lobby before they became static. They returned after fifty-eight seconds, catching the director running from the bathrooms to the scene of the crime—supposedly in response to the cries.

Crew members Bernard, Cathleen, and Mose were the first on the scene. They'd been in the workshop when the victim and accused entered with their argument. The three crew members expressed the awkwardness of overhearing the fight and hid behind a stage wall in the workshop. They hadn't seen William leave, and they heard Richard argue with someone up to the catwalk.

Richard's mom was also suspicious. Barbara Quigley normally dropped off her son at the playhouse, but that day she'd been called into work. Her alibi was too convenient. Plus, she believed in her husband's innocence enough to push their lawyer to hire an investigator. Maybe I was reading too much into it, but sometimes the party most convinced of the accused's innocence was the guilty party.

There were also reports of a thief at the theater. Cast and crew members claimed to have items stolen, misplaced, or broken. Security guards even heard someone wandering the theater house multiple times in previous nights. That broadened the suspect list to anyone off the streets if Richard had discovered the thief, then was killed for his knowledge.

Poirot floated behind me with a frown. "You mentioned that this was 'reserved' on the desk of the Head of Investigations?"

"That's what he said," I said, gesturing for him to wave the air just right to flip the next page.

"Fascinating," Sherlock said, whipping out a ghostly pipe. "Given the multitude of suspects and interviews, it appears that a considerable amount of leg-work has already been undertaken in this Case."

I subconsciously fidgeted with my bracelet in thought. "I suppose my first step tomorrow is to talk to the accused and the previous detectives and investigators who worked on this Case. Could you spread the word among the spirits? I'd like everyone who was present during the murder to be at the theater tomorrow night. I'll try to sleep there. Say what you will about my lack of resources, but I don't need living friends for this job. Only people to interview."

CHAPTER 3

The term "misjudged death" frequently arises with disguised suicides, intricately plotted accidents, or volleys caught in the crossfire. (To avoid looking "incompetent," make judgements with proof.)

> \- *Lemuel Gulliver's Travel Guide,*
> *Vol. 4: Mystery*
> (with notes by Aeron)

As soon as I woke, a curtain of fog covered half of my memory. Using techniques for remembering dreams, I remained still to review what I'd learned during the night, grasping for the details. How did it begin? The ending was usually the easiest to remember, though there was nothing significant. I did remember going to sleep with a desire to study and discuss the Case with my departed friends.

What I really needed was a spiritual note-taker. I needed a spirit with the gift of tangibility to take physical notes and communicate with the spirits while I was awake. Unfortunately, the gift of tangibility was incredibly rare and using it without permission from the higher-ups meant condemning their souls. I couldn't ask that of any of my friends.

As always, it was up to me to remember my dreams/spiritual visits. I reached to my nightstand and grabbed my Dream

Journal, then wrote down what I remembered most recently: Lestrade's spirit smiling at me from behind a pile of spirit scrolls. Were we in the town library? No, that wasn't quite right. There had been more filing drawers than bookshelves.

I closed my eyes and sat still, struggling to remember. It was like holding water with my hands. If it didn't seep through the cracks, it absorbed away through my skin.

Brief images flashed through my memories: of translucent people standing in my room, of reviewing the new Case. None of it stayed long enough to make sense, but I managed to recall a couple of keywords: interviews and connections.

I remembered the oddness of Mr. Baldi "reserving" this Case that had been passed through multiple investigators, and a desire to reach out to those investigators.

That thought felt familiar and right, giving me hope that I was on the right track.

I stood and went to my desk and the file papers. Looking over the reports jogged my memory of a few other thoughts from the night.

Silent Sleuth Services's client was Mr. Quigley's lawyer, meaning they hoped my investigation results would clear Mr. Quigley's name. However, with the police report against Mr. Quigley, he was guilty until proven innocent. With no verifiable alibi, it was much easier to prove a person guilty than to prove them innocent. That meant that the easiest way to prove Mr. Quigley was innocent of his son's murder was to find the real murderer. Supposing he wasn't the real murderer…

Who else could have murdered Richard Quigley? Mr. William Quigley was seen on the site of the crime, which meant there were other people present. That opened the suspect list to the cast and crew members of the playhouse.

A brief glance over the suspects and alibis sparked another memory from my spiritual visit. Out of the many pages of suspects, I pulled out the most suspicious: Director Stephens, Bernard, Cathleen, Mose, and Mr. and Mrs. Quigley.

There was also the minor unsolved Case of the unknown theater thief.

The death was almost written off as accidental. Young Quigley had landed on his head after a fifteen-foot fall from the catwalk. It was handed over to homicide when Bernard, Cathleen, and Mose (the auditory witnesses) claimed to hear Richard shouting before his fall.

It was definitely a puzzle. The more I read through the file, the more excited I became to solve it. If only I had more information.

"Connections."

That word stirred a memory. Something about a conversation from last night…

Agh! I couldn't remember. What kind of connections? Was there a connection in this Case? Connections between the incidents? Connections between the suspects? Connections… connections…

My clock alarm beeped.

Curses, my morning was spent, and I needed to prepare for my lunch appointment.

I had a meeting with Detective Kenneth Ross as he asked for my help on one of his Cases. Again.

I showered, enjoying the privacy in the one and only place where my spiritual friends left me alone. I dressed in my usual—dark slacks, black leather shoes, a white undershirt, and gray suit vest—then drove across town to the Shigaqua Police Station. But not exactly to the station. Det. Ross set our meeting at a bakery (WhoDonut) across the street from the station. Before I could crack any jokes about stereotypical cops with their donuts, I'd need to prove my worth beyond the stereotypical Cozy amateur sleuth with brains but no badge. Ross recognized my resources for information, but preferred to ignore me around others on the police force as if I was some dirty criminal informant.

Whatever. Such was my lot until I made myself known more as Ace of Spades than as Fantasy Freak. At least Ross occasionally let me borrow the police department's resources in return.

A little bell on the door announced my arrival as I stepped into WhoDonut. I spotted Ross at a little round table near the back. To my surprise and chagrin, he'd brought his partner, Detective Celso Montgomery.

Ross was a lean man for his early thirties with round eyes above his round nose and round mouth. Having never seen him without his fedora, I imagined him with permanent dark-brown hat-hair.

Montgomery, on the other hand, had a beer belly with a thin mouth, thin nose, and thin eyes. His square buzz-cut made him look like a shoebox with a bowtie set atop a pile of tires.

Ross waved to me as I approached. Montgomery raised his bottle-in-a-bag in greeting. They were almost ten years my senior, but only recently earned their stripes to become detectives in the police department.

"Hey, Digger," Ross said, using his personal nickname for me. He motioned for me to sit at their little table in the corner while Montgomery swayed on the edge of drunkenness.

"Montgomery's drunk already?" I asked, taking my seat.

Ross shook his head. "We had an all-nighter, searching for a perp who'll lead us to Sponsor."

"Really? That's huge!" As Shigaqua's leading mobster, taking down Sponsor would remove the resources of drugs and weapons to the major gangs in the area.

"You're telling me? The people who're gonna get all the credit are out there arresting the lead right now. We're clocked out and gonna go home after this."

"Good j—"

"Welcome!" Montgomery shouted from his slouched seat. "PI of Spades, the newest, youngest, Fantastic...-est inspector in town! D'you like cake? Normally, we share drinks with the newbies, but we ain't ever had someone under-age before."

I stared, confused, as Ross back-handed his partner. "Idiot. It was gonna be a surprise. Eh, anyway." He pulled up a Who-Donut cake box from the empty seat and set it on the table. "Congrats on your new job."

I smirked, warmed by his sentiment, but embarrassed that their celebrations were premature. The cake was a simple round of chocolate frosting. True to anything in Mystery, the inside flavors were unknown. I thanked them before they let me do the honors of cutting into it, revealing...pink.

"It's a girl!" Montgomery exclaimed, sloshing his drink. "But who's the mom?"

I took a bite and rolled teasing eyes. "It's strawberry, you dolt."

"Who says I'm a dolt?" he slurred. "I once passed the BAR, you know?"

"To go to the liquor store instead?" I asked.

"Hah," he barked without humor. "Like I ain't heard that one before?"

"Did you really need help with a Case," I asked Ross around another bite, "or can you help me with mine?"

"Naw, that request was a set-up," Ross said. "How else was I gonna get you here without suspecting a surprise celebration? But you already have a Case?"

"Yeah." The biggest surprise was his honest care. Then again, Ross and Montgomery looked for any excuse for cake. "But I'd like to discuss my new Case privately."

"Sure, sure." Ross grinned. "Hey, Montgomery, you wanna grab some water for us?" The man was drunk enough that simply standing and thinking of liquids made him waddle to the toilets.

"So," Ross asked around a bite of cake, "what's your Case?"

"First of all, thanks again for the celebrations, but I'm technically not a PI yet."

"What?"

"I'm not officially hired," I said. "Yet. Head Investigator Baldi gave me this Case to prove myself first."

I handed Ross the folder. He took a moment to stop gaping before he accepted the file. "Wha'd'ya mean he didn't hire you? You solve crime in your darned sleep like a freak! Is he a Mystery purist or something? How's he expect you to solve a Case without his agency's resources? What Case is it?"

"The Quigley murder," I said. "It's a criminal defense Case, and I have a week until he goes on trial."

"The—" Ross cut off as his jaw dropped. It bounced a couple of times on its way back up. "His trial's in a week? As in seven days? Digger, how do I say this? He rejected you."

"What?"

"This Case is dead. Like, dead done."

"I can deal with dead," I said.

Ross sighed. "You're still gonna try for it? You know, you don't hafta jump straight to the big leagues, right? I mean, nobody knew who William Quigley was until he was pinned for his son's murder, but he's still a B-lister in the movies. You don't hafta prove yourself to anybody."

I gave him a sideways glance. As if people would treat me differently by simply being a PI. No, I would always be a Fantastic. If I wanted people to treat me differently, I'd openly state my lineage. But I had to prove to myself and my parents that my aspirations to be a private investigator weren't a waste of time. At least, I hoped they weren't a waste of time. Solving a big Case like catching Sponsor would probably prove my worth.

I muttered, "I don't have time to work my way up to the big Cases."

Ross scoffed. "You're a decade ahead of the game, and you say you don't have time? What, are you gonna die or something?"

"No. Besides, I'm not afraid of death," I said. "I see it every night in my sleep."

No, I wasn't afraid of death. I was afraid of growing up. I was Peter Pan, living my own dreams in my own house in my own way.

Ross handed the file back to me, shaking his head. "Why did he reject you? Silent Sleuth Services has another Fantastic in the agency, so we can't call him a purist."

"He didn't reject me," I affirmed to him and myself. "He gave me a Case. And I'm going to prove to him and everyone out there that 'I ain't no chump to mess around.'"

Ross winced. "Didn't I tell you, you don't have the right accent to pull off that phrase?"

"Would you rather that I said I'm not a meater mutton shunter? I'm a podsnappery ready to shake a flannin."

He raised a slow eyebrow at me. "I have…no idea—what did you just say?"

"I don't know either," I laughed. "But I have a spirit friend who said it enough times one night that I remembered it after I woke up."

Ross joined my laughter, but faltered and inched away as the door rang with new customers from the police department. "You're serious about taking on the Quigley Case? You're gonna do it?"

"I have to try," I said, shifting to quickly scan the bakery's newest occupants. Four police officers and two civilian women approached the glass display and register. Of the two civilians, one was middle-aged, but the other was somewhere in her early twenties and…hard to define.

"You're insane, you know that?" Ross rambled. "Sorry, but this Case is outta my league. I can't help you. No one can find proof one way or the other. It's been set aside and collecting dust for months, but there might be someone else who can—Digger? You there?"

"Huh?" I blinked and failed to act like I'd listened the whole time.

He followed my distracted gaze to the young woman. "My word, Digger, are you still doing that?"

"Doing what?"

"Chasing after every skirt?"

"I don't chase every skirt," I defended. "I'm just…who is she?"

"Who knows?" he mumbled. "Come on, you wanna be introduced?"

"Do I?" I suddenly panicked.

"Actually, you do," Ross said. "You remember how I mentioned another Fantastic at Silent Sleuth Services? That's her, the older woman. That's PI Locke and her combat specialist, Ms. Incog. She was born in Fantasy, like you, but mostly raised in Mystery. Instead of talking to dead people, she can read palms. It's come in handy to identify victims and interview suspects. They're gonna help us on the Sponsor Case. More important to you, they were the last to work the Quigley Case. Don't you wanna get their input?"

"Yes, please." I'd already planned to look up the previous workers on the Case. Ross's introduction would save me time and give me a proper excuse to talk with the younger woman.

Montgomery returned from the restroom, but I didn't feel guilty about leaving him alone at the table. Ross stood and directed me to the older of the two women as the younger struggled to choose her food order. PI Locke wore an odd combination of a woman's trench coat over a multi-colored dress with several frayed layers like she couldn't decide whether to dress in business or casual. Her bulky jewelry clinked noisily with her every movement. Her eyes matched her mousy brown hair that frizzled outward and down her back.

"Aeron Spade," Ross said, "meet PI Truth Locke. Locke, this is Aeron Spade, or Digger as I like to call him. He's gonna wanna pick your brain about the—"

"Did you mean Aeron Fromm?" Truth Locke asked, and I tried not to panic. How did she know my real name? I'd expected PI Baldi to do a background check on me, but not this random and strange woman. "I heard you were coming to Noir," she continued, "but who'da thunk you'd come to Shigaqua?"

"Forgive me," I stammered, "have we met before?"

"Only now. Can you answer a question about your Case with the Smith treasure at The Boar? How did you learn the secrets of the treasure?"

She knew of me from my university projects? Sure, they'd been publicly published, but I hadn't expected anyone to actually read them. It also didn't explain how she knew my birth name. "I talked to the Smith's ancestors and the spirits at the bar," I said, hoping to slide past her usage of my real name.

"What kind of bar spirits now?" Montgomery joked from behind. He got a few chuckles from the other police, who joined the bakery for their lunch break.

Truth raised an eyebrow. "The ancestors? Were they still alive or are you a medium?"

"No, they're dead, I—"

I cut off as the younger woman stepped from behind Truth, holding their order of a paper bag with unknown contents. She also carried a steaming paper cup of herbal tea that she handed to Truth. Why did she strike my interest? She was pretty, but her features were plain. She didn't flaunt her muscled figure with revealing clothing or loud makeup, but her natural cleanliness spoke of careful hygiene. She wore an off-white blouse with a long muddy-brown skirt that seemed better for movement than fashion.

I'd courted women with hair as black as night, red as fire, brown as soil, or blonde as gold. This woman's hair was both blonde and brown, with hints of red in the right lighting. It was tied back in a tight bun, making its length indeterminable. Her skin tones were likewise undefinable. She was darker than my Fantastic father, but lighter than myself and my Horror mother. Was she multicultural too?

As she drew nearer, I amended my thoughts. It was definitely her eyes that caught my attention. Her eyes were blue violet one second, golden brown the next, then green and yellow, then back to blue. The shifts were subtle enough that I might have missed it without my analysis. I wanted to study them all day.

While distracted, Montgomery picked up my explanation. "Spade sleeps with dead people."

"Wha—I do not!"

My defenses to correct his crudeness were drowned in laughter from the surrounding police.

And that was why I worked better with the dead. To them, I was their speaker and advocate. They were my teachers and friends. They were my companions during the day and my tutors and counselors during the night.

Truth gave me an empathetic smile. "Most people don't understand the delicacy of speaking with the departed." She reached her hand over for a shake. "Abilities are frequently misunderstood, but I knew your parents at Heartford University."

Oh, curses. Oh. Curses! She hadn't heard about me from my university accomplishments or hadn't done a background check. It was far, far worse. She knew exactly who I was through my parents.

And what did I know of her? Truth Locke? She was the Fantastic hired by Silent Sleuth Services, but that was the extent of my knowledge. I scavenged my memory for any mention of her from my parents. Had they ever talked about a gypsy-looking private—

She gasped as if someone had dumped a bucket of ice water over her. An odd reaction to our handshake.

"What?" I asked. "Is something wrong?"

She didn't reply but took my hand with both of hers. She thumbed my palm and stared.

"Incredible!"

"What?" I asked, growing increasingly worried.

"Your hands are so decisive! Every line, every crease, every crisscrossing fold! It all points to death!"

I expected such an exclamation to be horrific, but Truth's tone was of pure excitement.

"Probably," I said, "because I spend a lot of time with the dead."

"Oh, I'm sure of it! That, or you'll die shortly. Within the week, I'd suppose."

I wiggled my hand from hers, suddenly feeling clammy. Fantastics like her were the reason Mysteries tended to avoid us. "Let's say it refers to my ability to interact with spirits in my dreams." I stole glances at the younger woman to see if she was impressed.

"We'll see soon enough. Supposing you get past the darkness, nice shooting." What the horror did she mean by that? "Also—" Truth tilted her head like a curious dog "—why do you keep glancing at my partner?"

The young woman finally showed interest in our conversation, and I fumbled.

"Glancing? I'm not glancing. Was I glancing?" If I hadn't been glancing, I was now. I was definitely glancing.

Truth smirked. "You're a terrible liar for an aspiring PI."

Her partner bore down on me. "Why were you staring at me? Do you know me?"

"What? No! We haven't met yet."

"Then why were you staring?"

"Because you're pretty!" I blurted.

Truth sighed in disappointment, and the younger woman frowned. Apparently, she wasn't the type to be flattered when told of her beauty. The land of Mystery liked to twist expectations, sure, but this conversation was on another level. Or maybe there was a hint of a surprised smile on her shapely lips.

"If you haven't met," Truth said, "this is Nita, my working partner and combat specialist."

My brain shouted at me to stop staring like an idiot. I shouted back for it to say something clever.

"Sorry," I said, "I'm not used to talking with…people. All my friends are dead."

And so were my hopes for a date.

My smidgen of a mojo screamed at me to shut up. I didn't listen.

"So, um, after work, would you like to go—"

"No," Nita said.

"You didn't even let me finish."

"I don't need to hear it," she said. "I don't date investigators."

"Oh? That slims your pickings in this town." I attempted to smirk between my flustering. "Besides, I was going to ask if you wanted to go out for a drink, just to get to know each other. That's not a date, and it definitely wouldn't mean we were dating."

"Forgive me, I wasn't clear," she said. "I don't date, go out, or hang out with people. I prefer to keep my relationships professional."

Ross chuckled and took his seat by Montgomery. "You're gonna find that difficult here. Digger likes to be chummy."

"Yeah, you two are tight," Montgomery laughed, "like Spade's buttocks."

I happened to be standing with my back toward a policewoman. She spewed her coffee across her table.

Montgomery laughed. "Caught you looking, Taylors!"

Taylors blushed deeply and put extra attention into cleaning her coffee mess.

Ross scoffed. "We're not nearly that tight."

I scowled at him. So much for pretending to be my friend earlier. That was before other police officers arrived.

"Actually, PI Locke," I said, "I could use your help for my first Case. I've been assigned the Quigley Case, and I heard you two were the last to work on it."

With my mention of the Quigley Case, the WhoDonut went silent enough to hear the hum of the bakery's back refrigerators.

"Wait...what?" Taylors asked.

Montgomery sided to Taylors, "Are we taking bets? I think the freaky Ace of Spades finally met his match."

I caught myself fiddling with my leather bracelet and forced myself to stop. "Please?" I asked Truth. "I'd appreciate your insight."

She beamed. "I'd love to see how the Haunted works."

I coughed, hoping no one heard her casual drop of my homeland nickname. Curse her if she was the death of my alias. Mysteries already treated me differently because of my Fantastic origins and spiritual ability. I hated to imagine how they'd treat me if they knew about my lineage on top of everything else.

I beckoned the women to join me outside. The whispering gossip started even before the door shut completely.

"PI Locke, people in Mystery don't know me by my Fantasy names or lineage. I'd prefer to keep it that way."

She crossed her arms and tapped her chin. "Are you ashamed of your parents?"

"No, I just want a clean slate in Mystery. Will you help me with the Quigley Case or not?"

Nita's stoic stare became, if possible, more hardened. "The Quigley Case is a waste of time. Mr. Quigley and his wife can claim innocence all they want, but they must be lying. There's no other explanation for his son's death, unless it was an accident."

"I don't know," Truth said, tapping her chin again. "Based on my reading of him, Mr. Quigley had a guilty conscience, but it wasn't fresh. He honestly and truthfully loved his son. I wanted to keep working on it, but Baldi pulled us off so we could assist the police with the Sponsor Case."

I allowed myself to be jealous of their position on the Sponsor Case before refocusing on the interesting additions to the Quigley Case. That was exactly the type of information I hoped to glean from them. What other insights did they hold outside of the record?

"Please," I said, "I'll let you keep the reward money. I just need to close this Case."

Truth's eyebrows went up, but Nita's dropped down in a subtle frown.

"What's your angle?" the young woman asked. "If you're not in it for the money, why's this Case so important to you?"

Stepping closer, I lowered my voice. "I'd rather not disclose it to the world, but my hire at Silent Sleuth Services hinges on closing this Case. I need to do this, but I don't have clearance or the agency's resources. I'd really appreciate any extra insights you have about this Case."

"Hmm," Truth mused. "The first thing you ought to know about the Quigleys is they've been passed on a lot. Multiple detectives were involved in solving the murder, but the dad refused to confess, and the mom was convinced of his innocence. So, their lawyer reached out to the SSS, but nobody could find another viable suspect to create reasonable doubt. By the time Nita and I met with them, they were tired of meeting new detectives and retelling their alibis. There were several people at the scene, but no one actually witnessed the murder. It doesn't help that the victim had no friends. He was a hateful teenager, and a loner at that. He wasn't malicious, but he didn't care for his place in the theater and made sure everyone knew it."

"Great," I muttered. "Is there a chance you could introduce me to the Quigleys? If they've been passed around a lot, a smooth transition with a referral from you will help them to work with me."

Also, I wouldn't mind spending a bit more time testing Nita's smile.

"Of course," Truth said. "Since his trial's at the end of the week, I assume the sooner the better. I'll make some calls and get back to you with a time."

Perfect. Even if I was surrounded by the stereotypical "incompetent cops" like a Cozy, at least I gained the benefit of a "detective team-up."

CHAPTER 4

In matters of adult homicides, the accusatory finger
invariably points towards the partner of romance.
(It's always the lover!)

-    *Lemuel Gulliver's Travel Guide,*
Vol. 4: Mystery
(with notes by Aeron)

Mrs. Barbara Quigley turned out to be available that afternoon. With her husband's trial that week, I imagined she was anxious to meet with her lawyer's hired investigators. I said thanks and farewell to Det. Ross before following Truth and Nita to the Quigley home. They used the elevated rails that ran through the city, but I used any excuse to drive my car, even if the weather forced me to put up my convertible top. The usual city rain came down at a harsh angle. It would likely turn into a summer storm at nightfall.

Like many of Shigaqua's downtown residents, Mrs. Quigley lived in a boxy apartment building with too many floors and too little soundproofing against the elevated tracks. I found parking underground, then took the stairs to the eleventh floor. As much as I hated stairs, I hated elevators more. I blamed my mom for ingraining that Horror paranoia in me. Whatever. Stairs were healthier, right?

Huffing, I found Truth and Nita waiting for me in the hallway. Healthier maybe, but definitely slower.

Truth let me catch my breath before knocking on the door, then stepped back. A woman answered, opening the door only a crack until she saw Truth, then unlatched the chain to welcome us. Accurately depicted in the Case file, Mrs. Quigley was in her early forties with light brown eyes. Her blonde hair was cut at a bob and she wore a simple floral dress with round lapels.

"Oh, Ms. Locke," she said. "Do you have news about my son's Case? Come in, sit down. Do you want something to drink?"

"Tea would be fine," Truth said, leading Nita and me into the home. In a word, the apartment reminded me of rust. Displaying Noir's standard fashion, the walls were muted brown to compliment the muddy-brown carpet, and the curtains were sepia yellow to contrast with the sun-bleached blue armchair and rustic red couch. Even though the place was clean, it smelled of dust and old-fashioned pot-pourri. The living room centered around a boxy color television with antennae that poked two feet into the air. One of the new-tech TV remotes rested on the coffee table.

Between Mr. Quigley's B-list acting and Mrs. Quigley's job at the laundromat, they had established themselves on the higher end of middle-class. I didn't see much else as three wooden doors leading to other rooms were closed. A cutout archway in the wall let me spy into the flower-themed kitchen with pale yellow appliances.

Truth sat on the couch with practiced ease while Nita stood like a posted guard against the side wall. Ah, from there, she had a clear view of every door. I joined Truth on the couch, taking note of the indentation of the cushion. Someone had spent a lot of time lounging there. Mr. Quigley?

With the kettle warming on the stove, Mrs. Quigley returned to sit primly in the armchair close to Truth. Based on the basket of knitting projects beside the chair, I assumed that was her usual spot. This was a home of order and routines, but the question remained; whose order and routines? The dad's, mom's, or both?

Mrs. Quigley wiped her hands down her skirts and asked Truth, "Did you find something to save my husband?"

"Not quite," Truth said. "Your Case has been reassigned, so I wanted to introduce you to the new investigator."

Mrs. Quigley shook her head before Truth even finished. "No," she said. "I don't want anyone else. We've been reassigned four times already. Four! And as many times as I've had to recount everything that happened, you were the only one who took us seriously and didn't push my husband and me as suspects. I know the whole Case is strange, but I will swear on my life that my husband and I are innocent. We loved our boy and never would've done anything to hurt him. This whole thing has been difficult enough. I can't handle another stuffed badge poking his head into our lives and accusing us of things we didn't do!"

"Barbara," Truth said with a calming hand, "we're not here to accuse you. We want to get to the bottom of this just as much as you do. We have your new handler here, and if he doesn't respect you with all the love and personal care that I gave you, I'll report him to his superior immediately."

I almost smirked at the fact that I didn't currently have a superior since Mr. Baldi hadn't hired me yet. Still, if he heard that I mistreated a client, it would hurt my reputation more than simply failing to solve their Case. Also, there was the terrifying thought that Truth knew my parents. Mr. Baldi was her superior, not mine, and she hadn't said "our" superior…

Eager to divert my thoughts, I leaned forward in my seat and accepted Truth's gesture of introduction. "Mrs. Quigley," I began, "My name is Aeron Spade. Similar to PI Locke, I'm originally from Fantasy and have a special ability that helps me to solve difficult Cases."

"My husband's trial is next week! How can you possibly solve my son's murder with so little time when others have tried and failed these past five months?"

I sat straight in my chair and met her gaze without blinking. "I have an ability."

"So does she." Mrs. Quigley gestured at Truth.

"His ability's different from mine," Truth said. "While my ability lets me look into people's lives and personalities, his ability lets him talk with the dead directly."

"What, like in a séance? We don't need a psychic. I thought that was what you were," she said, pointing at Truth. "Now you're passing us to this boy? Forgive me, but you look only a few years older than my son."

"Aeron," Truth said, "maybe you should tell her what exactly it is that you do?"

"I enter the spirit realm in my sleep," I said as my most basic explanation. "I may talk with your son face-to-face and ask him directly about his murder."

Mrs. Quigley's eyes screwed into confusion. "That's… wrong. What is it with you Fantasy f—Fantastics that defies all logic and reasoning? How do you expect that to hold up in court? The jury won't believe the testimony of a ghost."

"No, they won't," I said. "But it's a lot easier to find evidence when you know what to look for. I promise to discover the real murderer and prove their guilt to put them away."

Somewhere from the back of my mind, I recalled my mom's warning to "never make promises." I ignored it. If I couldn't solve this Case, I'd have bigger issues than any fallout from a broken promise.

Mrs. Quigley stared hard at me as she worked her jaw side to side in thought. "If you can actually do that, I'll double whatever my lawyer's paying you. What do you need from me?"

"First," I said, "I need you to tell me everything you know about your son's death."

With a heavy sigh, she began her side of the story, which, unfortunately, didn't reveal anything new outside of the reports.

I asked question after question to fish for new information about her son, the theater, and its occupants, but she hadn't been at the theater during her son's death. She'd been at work (with two coworkers as her witnesses) and hadn't learned about the accident until her son was proclaimed dead and they called next of kin.

I struggled not to fidget with my bracelet during the interview. Truth mostly consoled Mrs. Quigley between sips of tea while Nita lurked behind like a pacing panther. Either the apartment had a major leak or a kitchen window was left open as I heard the pitter-pattering of rain grow heavier. Interviews weren't normally this long, but I wanted to be thorough. This was also my first Case, and a rushed one at that. There had to be more than what the reports said, and I didn't have time for follow-up interviews.

I begrudgingly admitted a small egotistical desire to impress Nita with my interviewing skills. One of those skills was also not to take more time than needed. I considered wrapping up my interview when a thought like a spiritual guidance entered my mind. *Ask her about the theater.*

Had that been one of my ghostly friends communicating with me?

"Mrs. Quigley," I asked, "do you have any other experiences related to the Regal Theater?"

"Of course," she said. "We were benefactors. It's a non-profit theater meant to support the arts community and offer amateurs a chance for a big stage. Though Bill and I rarely attended—you know how life can be—he always purchased season tickets and sent a quarterly donation."

She stood to open a closet door to retrieve a small framed black and white photo, lightly browned with age.

"See? There I am." She pointed at a teenage version of herself in the middle of a dozen others. A man on the edge—the director?—held a framed photo of a young man. Maybe he hadn't been able to attend the photoshoot. Mrs. Quigley pointed to a grinning boy with his arm around her shoulders. "Bill and I were in lead roles and started dating during the show."

Her smile turned sad, and she looked away from the photo.

"Bill kept this photo on his desk."

I frowned at her wording. "Kept? When did he remove it?"

"He didn't." She squirmed. "I did. After he was arrested. Any reminder of that horrid playhouse makes me feel gross inside."

Not after her son died there? I considered their interactions, implications, and the possibilities. The photographic reminder of glory days and young love for Mr. Quigley haunted Mrs. Quigley. But she'd waited until Mr. Quigley was gone before removing it. The reasons were too variable to make any solid theories.

I studied the face of Mr. William Quigley in the picture. His teenage boy expression was one of a champion—a little exhausted, but elated. He was someone who worked hard to earn the victory that he expressed during the picture.

"Thank you, Mrs. Quigley," I said, handing over the picture. "I'll do everything I can to put your son's soul to rest. May I contact you again if I need a follow-up interview?"

"That should be fine," Mrs. Quigley said. We shook hands and started toward the door.

Bang!

Mrs. Quigley screamed.

I jumped for cover behind the sofa, tackling Nita to the ground with me.

Mrs. Quigley muttered an expletive as her voice traveled into the kitchen. "Dagnabbit. Looks like a storm's coming in. It blew over a vase. Sorry, there's nothing to worry about… Just a crack. Ma will be distraught, but no doubt she'll give me another one, anyway."

Eased by her explanation, I became aware of my position on the floor. Nita's body was pinned beneath my own with our legs tangled from my tackle. She looked up at me with wide eyes that morphed from brown to green. Her cheeks slowly reddened as I stared.

Right, I wasn't supposed to be staring. I was supposed to be standing. I raised myself to one knee and offered a hand to help her. She refused my hand and wouldn't meet my eyes. I stood and repeated my condolences to the grieving mother.

As soon as Mrs. Quigley shut the door behind us, Nita exploded.

"What the crapshoot was that, Spade? Care to explain yourself?"

I cleared my throat. "I heard a bang and thought to protect you."

"Protect me?" she scoffed. "From what? The vase? When I 'heard a bang,' I didn't bother reacting because I'd heard it wobbling earlier. I was prepared for the disturbance and had already assessed it as harmless. Even if there had been a danger, your reaction was delayed and poorly executed. I can protect myself," she snapped. "Out of the three of us, I'm probably the best at protecting myself and others."

Truth nodded. "There's no 'probably' about that."

Nita continued, "Even if we were in danger, I'm the last person anyone should protect."

"Ah—"

"Wha—"

"No," Nita mowed over both of our arguments. "I have deeper training than you two to protect myself. Also, I'm nobody special. No—Truth, let me finish. You're a psychic, for goodness' sake! And you're—" She paused as she turned her accusation on me. "Well, you're something else. I don't really know what you are, but nobody else can do what you two do. Protect me," she spat. "I'm supposed to be the one protecting you guys. People depend on you to do your jobs, so you guys can depend on me to do mine."

Truth and I waited in silence to be sure she was done ranting at us. I didn't know Nita had the capability of saying so many words at once. Even more, I wasn't sure how to respond, so I stayed quiet as they turned down the hallway to the elevator. Sure, she was oddly striking, but maybe I'd bitten off more than I could chew with that woman.

Either way, I'd be better off focusing on the Case.

Statistically, murders were most committed by scorned lovers. There was a reason for the saying, "It's always the spouse." Richard's youth and single-status debunked that option, but to kill someone on purpose required a relationship with the victim, familiarity with the setting, and access to the lethal weapon (in this case, the catwalk).

Mrs. Quigley hadn't told me much I didn't already know, but analyzing her tidy—yet lived in—home, watching her move about her house, and observing her mannerisms as she talked about the theater confirmed a few assumptions.

First, Mrs. Quigley was either truly innocent or a masterful actress and schemer. Sure, she once had a leading role at the theater, but considering her solid alibi, I leaned toward innocence. Second, she firmly believed in her husband's innocence. She had pushed her lawyer to hire investigators (leading to me) to prove it.

If nothing else, I'd learned a little more about the Quigley's relationship to the scene of the crime. While Mrs. Quigley despised the theater, Mr. Quigley had a deep fondness for it as the place where he'd met his wife. Keeping the photo despite their son's death implied that Mr. Quigley valued his golden days over the loss of his own son.

I needed to meet Mr. Quigley and survey that theater. Thankfully, Truth had scheduled an appointment with the prison to introduce me to Mr. Quigley tomorrow. That gave me time to have a sleepover at the scene of the crime.

CHAPTER 5

Primary motives for the act of murder encompass, yet are
not confined to, an insatiable greed for possessions not
rightfully theirs, vainglory of claimed belongings, and a
wrath provoked by the actions of others.
(The 7 deadly sins are "deadly" after all.)

- *Lemuel Gulliver's Travel Guide,*
Vol. 4: Mystery
(with notes by Aeron)

Shigaqua was a big city with several theaters, including some fancy color-film theaters. The scene of Richard Quigley's murder, however, was a small playhouse outside of downtown, suited more for volunteers than fancy red carpet actors.

I found a parking spot across the street of the Regal Theater with switch-out letters announcing the upcoming performance of "The Mousetrap." No one sat in the ticket booth, but the lights were on. Trying the doors, I found one unlocked and slipped into the foyer, out of the rain.

No, this wasn't a red carpet theater. The carpet was a hideous floral of oranges and greens with posters of previous performances decorating its pink wallpapered walls. I followed the sound of voices into the auditorium. The vomit-inspired carpet continued down the aisles, clashing with enough teal blue seats for an audience of about a hundred. There was an upper balcony with about thirty more seats, but no private box seats. The orchestra pit was merely a half-walled section in front of the stage that was currently occupied with a few teenagers and a couple of adults painting a fake wall to look like a manor house interior with winter themes.

One of the adults snapped his fingers at a high school boy who seemed to be talking to himself. "Major…Major…Major Metcalf!" With an annoyed sigh, the man said, "John!" The boy jumped, suddenly alert. "I'm talking to you. You need to learn to respond to your character's name. Also, you're practicing your lines like a police officer interrogating Mrs. Boyle. You're spoiling the ending! The audience only knows you're ex-military and nosey like a Cozy."

The boy frowned with concentration as he tried to imagine the scene, then said, "Yes, Director."

Ah, the director was a good place to start for interviews. I walked down the aisle and waved when he noticed me.

"Who are you?" he asked. "If you're looking for a tryout, come back in August. You have the looks for a good role in next season's 'The Man Who Knew Too Much.'"

"Thanks," I said, "but I'm here to investigate the death of Richard Quigley." He didn't look like Director Stephens— Richard's director, leading me to ask, "Did you take over for Stephens?"

"I teach theater at Clue High School, but I took the director position for this season to keep the Regal from going under. This place used to be the biggest thing in town, if you can believe it."

"Is that so?" I asked, admiring the lowered lighting fixtures. Not that I could tell the difference between one light from the next, but I mentally noted how the upkeep had ignored the carpet.

"You bet," the director continued. "They even got some decent upgrades like the catwalk and rehearsal room, thanks to the benefactors. But after the murder…" He scanned the stage and seating with eyes that cried goodbye. "Stephens held true to the saying, 'the show must go on,' but as soon as they finished 'Dial M for Murder,' he went dark. Losing an actor on set is a career killer and not just for the victim. A real pity. Stephens was a master of the theater."

"I see," I said. That opened the possibilities of motive. Someone might have killed Richard simply to oust Director Stephens. Rash, yes, but possible. "What do you know about Richard's death?"

"It was the Regal Ghost!"

We both turned toward the eavesdropping interrupter: a young blond boy with braces and more acne than chest hair.

The director sighed dramatically. "There's no such thing as the Regal Ghost."

"If you don't believe in the ghost, then why do you flip out any time someone says Macbeth?"

"Pearson!" the director shouted. "Outside! Now! Turn around three times, then knock three times! You're not allowed back into this playhouse until someone invites you in! Now, go!"

Pearson ducked his head and scampered to the back of the stage, presumably to a back exit.

"So," I drawled, "do you believe in ghosts or not?"

His anger slightly dissipated when he faced me again. "The Scottish Play isn't a ghost, but a curse. I like to keep myself grounded on facts, but I'm not dumb enough to test theories. Anyone who works in theater knows that accidents happen. Sometimes, it's nice to have something to blame, even if it sounds superstitious. It doesn't help that every theater is required to have a light on the stage even when it's not in use, and you know what they call it? The ghost light. Go figure. The kids say the light is for the ghosts. But what can I say? We're thespians. We're artists of illusions to make the impossible believable."

"Fair enough," I said. "Who would I talk to about staying the night as part of my investigation?"

The director raised an eyebrow. Yes, I knew it was an odd request, but it was one that I frequently made during my Cases. I could travel through walls in my sleep, but I couldn't blink and appear somewhere like Hercule Poirot. Sleeping at crime scenes saved travel time and gave me physical access to otherwise private areas.

"Security usually shows up around nine as we're leaving," the director said. Figures. He handed me off to someone else to answer my question. "They usually lounge around the backstage office and green room. Can't tell you how they'll respond to your overnight request."

"Thanks," I said. If the cast and crew had all switched out since Richard's play, I figured my most effective interviews would be with the dead. I still had an hour before the overnight security showed up, so I left to find a quick dinner. Feeling ravenous, I picked up a burger with mystery meat (turned out to be a sausage burger), some potato side (cross-cut fries), and milk. I needed to sleep well, and I doubted the theater kept any real mattresses. That meant I needed comfort foods to make myself sleepy. I grabbed a second meal to share with the security to get on their good side. Who needed bribes when one could use charm?

I returned with enough time to tour the theater. There were public bathrooms off the lobby, but the rest of the theater was backstage. Behind the stage was a long hallway parallel to the stage. A door on the far left led to a large room with scripts and markers taped all across the floor. A rehearsal room? The next room down the hallway led to a room crowded with costumes, wigs, hats, and all the fixings. Next, I passed two dressing rooms that included a wall of tables, chairs, and mirrors, plus washrooms. Nearing the right side of the hallway, the next door opened into what I presumed was the green room. It wasn't green, but more like a studio apartment with a small fridge, a microwave and sink, a water cooler, a small table with a few chairs, and a lounging couch. I stored the extra meal in the refrigerator and continued my personal tour.

The door to the green room swung easily with years of use. Right next to it, at the end of the long hallway, was a locked door. I'd ask security for help with that later.

Continuing my path counter-clockwise, I went back to the stage and through an extra wide door for loading. This room was full of past set structures, costumes, and a large locker labeled "Props." A green "Exit?" sign lit the backdoor beside a larger loading door. Peeking through put me in a typical alley, paved ages ago and wide enough for a single vehicle between the boring brick backside of shops, businesses, and a couple of houses on the other side.

Back on stage but behind the fake walls, yellow caution tape roped off the spiral staircase access to the catwalk and overhead lighting. It seemed to be in the process of removal. That usually happened to crime scenes.

I hunched to make myself Richard's height of five-foot-three, then looked up at the catwalk and around myself. The scene didn't look any different, but it was among the last sights of Richard's life. What did he see that made him go up the catwalk? He was a cast member, not crew. According to the report, none of his fellow cast members had seen him up there before. As far as anyone knew, Richard didn't know how to work the lights, and "Dial M for Murder" didn't require the catwalk.

Others had overheard him arguing with his father earlier, but that would have been close to the back entrance. Even if their argument traveled dozens of feet to where I stood, why would Richard go up the catwalk? It wasn't a place to hide. My uncle's Horror survival book correctly warned that "Running upstairs to escape will only get you trapped," though few in Mystery had read Horror's number one bestseller. Had Richard gone up there to meet with someone? If so, who?

I caught the heavy screech of the back door opening. Witnesses had heard Richard arguing with his father. Had they heard him leave with that noisy door?

I went to greet the newcomer, happy to find my assumption correct; it was the security.

"Hello," I said, reaching for a handshake.

"Hello?" he said with a heavy Mystery accent, taking my hand with curiosity.

"My name is Aeron Spade. I'm working with Silent Sleuth Services to investigate the murder of Richard Quigley."

The night shift security stared at me with wide eyes. "Weren't there two ladies working on that Case?"

"Locke and Incog? They've been helpful with the transition. Feel free to call and confirm with them. I'd show you my badge, but unfortunately, I was only brought into the firm yesterday and haven't received my official documents yet." That was true enough. "Actually, do you like Burglar Burgers?"

"Yeah," he said, his Mystery accent asking where I was going with my question.

"I ordered more than I needed for dinner. There's an extra meal in the green room fridge if you'd like it." His eyes shifted in the direction of the green room, and I plowed forward. "Speaking of the green room, may I spend the night on the couch as part of my investigation? I don't plan to be a nuisance. I'll go right to sleep. Worst-case scenario, I turn out to be a bum you let sleep in the theater for one night."

"Uh huh," he said, eyeing me with suspicion. "You know this place is haunted, right?"

So was I. I smirked. "I've heard about the Regal Ghost. I'm eager to meet them."

Apparently, he thought I was teasing him as he became defensive. "Look, I know this ain't Paranormal, and I was skeptical too, but then I started working here. How else do my cameras have a static attack right as something moves or goes missing? What else makes the doors open and close on their own? I hear moans or music playing, but when I go to check—"

I raised my hand to stop him. "I'm well acquainted with spirits and their pastimes."

He narrowed his eyes on me. "Then are you one of those ghost hunters? Look, I've been working around this theater for years, and they don't mean no trouble. I mind my own business, and they mind theirs. If you go around stirring up trouble—"

"No trouble," I said. "I just want to talk with them and help rest their souls."

His expression didn't change, but he motioned for me to follow him. "Are you good with the couch in the green room?"

"Yes, thank you," I said. "If you don't mind, I'd like to do some of my own security checks after the thespians leave. Could you show me what's behind the locked door in the hallway?"

He scoffed and waved a hand to say he wouldn't bother with arguing. He'd probably had to deal with a number of detectives and investigators ever since Richard's death. He directed me to the single locked door and opened it. Inside, the back office security room was furnished with filing cabinets, a desk, a chair, and five CCTV screens. They showed a wide angle of the front lobby, the back door and loading bay leading to the alley, the hallway, the stage from a back angle (the catwalk out of sight), and the rehearsal room.

No cameras in the dressing rooms. Yay for privacy. Boo for blind spots. Still, it was a decent setup for a little old theater. Just how much did their benefactors donate?

"Let me guess," I said, "the cameras revealed nothing about Richard's murder?"

He nodded. "That day, big Quigley walked into the loading bay with little Quigley. Who needs sound when their body language was enough to tell they were arguing? Then, fifty-eight seconds of static. Every camera went berserk. I was checking on the closest one in the hallway when the screams rang out. The cameras came back on without a hitch, and the little Quigley was dead on center stage."

The testimony corroborated with his recorded statement and the transcriptions of the security feeds. I thanked him, then went to work in the green room.

I prepared my bedding on the couch with a simple pillow and blanket while waiting for the cast and crew to finish their session. I couldn't let them distract me during my work.

After a decade of tests, I understood my ability's limits. I required two hours of sleep before entering the spirit realm. If someone or something woke me in the middle of the night, it cost me an extra two hours to return to the spirit realm. I wanted this done tonight, which meant no distractions.

After the director left, leaving me alone with the security, I made my own rounds to check that everything was in order. All the doors and windows were locked. I checked with the security and the cameras pointing at the doors. I also arranged some minor tripwires to capture any intruders. If there was a thief sneaking around the playhouse at night, I'd catch them.

With everything settled, I arranged myself on the couch.

Then, my least favorite time: the moment I turned off the lights. My heartbeat picked up despite the baton flashlight in my left hand. The night was dark, rain continued to pound on the window and roof, and was that a draft in the air? I flashed my baton light at the window and door to the hallway again to check. Closed tight. My heartbeat throbbed in my head.

Calm down. Breathe. Maybe the draft was from one of my spiritual friends?

My hands shook in the darkness as I rearranged my bedding.

I did my best to relax on the couch. Pillow puffed and covering my baton light, I curled up on the cushions between the two armrests that were too short for my five-foot and eleven-inches.

Failing to fall asleep was frustrating, and the fact that I was frustrated kept me from sleeping. I slowed my breathing and measured it. In for four seconds, hold for seven seconds, then out for eight seconds.

Inhale, 2, 3, 4. Hold, 2, 3, 4, 5, 6, 7. Exhale, 2, 3, 4, 5, 6, 7, 8...

A creak of wood in the hallway broke my silent meditation. I was used to such creaks in my own house. But I wasn't in my own house. It didn't help that I felt someone watching me. Maybe someone really wanted to talk with me.

"I can't talk with you," I mumbled, "until I fall asleep, and I can't sleep if I think someone's watching. The sooner I relax, the sooner I can join you."

No response, and the unsettling feeling remained. The glass window hummed from the wind rushing down the alley. I focused on keeping calm and comfortable despite the dark and unknown room.

I did a breathing exercise, but a stupid song played on a loop through my mind. I didn't even know all the lyrics. Just the peppy tune and big-band rhythms. I tried to sing a different song in my head. A lullaby. One that Aunt Di taught me years ago.

> Your thoughts of sweet sleep stretch your
> dreams to the sky.
> You'll build your own boats and you'll learn
> how to fly.
> Sail farther than ever and soar just as high.

I tried my breathing exercise again with the lullaby. I measured my breathing again, counting with each inhale, hold, then exhale.

In, hold…out… In, hold…out…

Two hours later, my spirit rose from my body. My vision was brighter as a spirit, alleviating my fears of the dark. I saw the world as if every night was a cloudless full moon despite the roof and rain. I looked around myself, surprised by the empty green room. I was alone.

Why was I alone? At least one or two spirits always waited for me the moment I came to visit them. They always had questions or updates for me. Where were they? Didn't they know that I needed help with this Case? I needed their eyes and senses to figure out what really happened here.

"Hello?" I asked aloud. No response.

But there was a sound in the distance.

"Hello?" I asked again, drifting through the door, toward the sounds. They came from the rehearsal room at the end of the hallway. Why did it seem to stretch and grow farther away as I slowly drifted closer? How did the sounds grow louder without becoming defined with distinction? Finally, I made it to the rehearsal door and slipped through.

The stories about the theater being haunted were true. I wasn't surprised. Ghosts enjoyed theatrics as much as the living. Perhaps more so, because they no longer needed to slave away at work, they finally had time for entertainment. They could change costumes on a whim, and some spirits had a gift to multiply themselves, filling an entire cast with their own one-man show. Also, flying like Peter Pan or Mary Poppins was easier, with no strings attached.

Emotional dialogue called across the rehearsal room while music played on repeat to practice a phrase. An entire cast of spirits practiced like they were on the biggest stage in town. Eight replications of one woman created a dancing crew that pranced in a ballet routine. Two more practiced a duet by the upright piano while a colonial director instructed a leadman through his lines.

Above all else, the director shouted, "Nay, nay! With fervor! Thy soulmate hath rent thy heart and flung it to the dogs! Once more!"

Directors were always good people for information, so I approached the shouting man wearing a crinkled collar, puffy tunic, and tights.

"Excuse me? Is Richard Quigley still in the house? He died here during this last winter."

The director rolled his eyes, irritated at my interruption, but answered, "The young thespian who met his demise on center stage? Nay. He hath departed hence to tarry with his forebears."

His forebears—so Richard's spirit was linked to his parents. His mom or dad? Unfortunately, being linked didn't tell me whether he watched over them with love or to haunt them. Then I'd need to visit his mom's home or dad's prison to find him. Normally, I'd ask Poirot to blink there and blink back with the witness like a spiritual subpoena. Without him, I'd waste time traveling. Might as well inspect the theater while I was there.

Addressing the room of ghosts, I asked, "Did anyone witness his death?"

"It is believed that Mr. Neil beheld the grim fall," the director said. "He doth oft frequent the shadowed corners before the stage, where he doth bemoan his fate. Such is our cause for utilizing the rehearsal hall."

Three copies of the dancing spirit echoed, "Beware the pits."

"What?" I asked. "Why?"

They ignored me as if they hadn't said anything, but continued dancing.

That was ominous. I thanked them and let myself sink through the door to the stage.

True to the living director's words, a single blue light bathed the empty stage. The ghost light.

Moaning caught my attention. I followed the sound to a ghost wandering in the orchestra pit among ghostly bloody chairs and music stands. He appeared in his late fifties, floating around the orchestra pit. He had short white hair, a pale complexion (even for a ghost), and square facial features with light blue eyes. He wore a tattered general's cloak over a broken suit of armor. Odd. Usually, ghosts liked to put on the ritz since they could change with the blink of an eye, and the only limit to their apparel was their own imagination.

Did he wear a costume? Why? Which character did he play? A costume wouldn't tell me which era he died in. He stared around at his bloody surroundings as if he was lost.

"Excuse me, sir," I said. "My name is Aeron Spade. I'm visiting from the living and investigating the death of young Richard Quigley. Can you tell me—"

His moaning cut short, and he noticed me. He charged at me with his nose flared, eyes wide in sunken wells, and fingers bent like claws.

What the horror?

First of all, why did this spirit hate me with such venom? Second, spirits didn't attack other spirits since they simply passed through each other. Didn't he know that he was dead?

I remained firmly in place, curious for his reaction. He slipped right through me and stumbled into a nightstand prop before he turned to stop.

Hold on…he stumbled into a nightstand?

He reached for the skull prop on top and lifted it.

He had the gift of tangibility!

He threw the prop, and it soared through my face. It smacked against the fake wall behind me, tipping it backwards into the next one as the fake skull bounced across the floor.

I flew across the stage, back to better lighting in the hallway. The ghost didn't care. Zipping through the walls, I hoped to lose the spirit, but he kept pace with me. I made it to the green room, but…then what? All I did was lead the ghost to a living stranger slumbering on the couch. The ghost's focus shifted to my tangible form.

Gritting his teeth, he charged again, this time at my body.

"No!" I closed my eyes and willed myself to wake. It didn't work. I rarely woke early without the aid of an alarm. The spirit grabbed for my body, and I felt his fingers around my neck.

Wake up!

<hr>

I woke, shaking, sweating, and throwing my body against the back of the couch. Someone had grabbed me. I still felt the imprint of a hand on my throat, but I was alone in the room. I fingered my neck to make sure nothing was there despite the recent choking sensation.

I swallowed heavily, feeling my Adam's apple beat with the weight of my stomach. Grabbing my dream journal, I wrote down the single terrifying thought that I remembered from my sleep.

"Poltergeist."

CHAPTER 6

There exists a certain analogy betwixt a cat and a mouse, yet amidst the intricate dance betwixt detective and villain, the roles of the feline and the rodent may interchange. (Think like a cat, act like a cat, be a cat)

- *Lemuel Gulliver's Travel Guide,
Vol. 4: Mystery*
(with notes by Aeron)

The security burst into the green room, livid and terrified.

"What the burning blazes did you do?" he shouted. "The stage camera went on the fritz, then I hear a crash like the world's coming down! I told you not to stir any trouble!"

I ignored him, grabbed my bedding, and pushed past him. There was no way I was staying in that theater for the rest of the night. No way.

I high-tailed it out of there, not bothering to properly pack my security tools or to change from my sleeping clothes for the rain.

Jumping into my car, I drove away, praying to the gods of Fantasy and supernaturals of Horror. "Don't let it follow me. Don't let it follow me. Stop it from following me." Desperate,

I shouted, "If you're following me, you'd better stop! I'm on my way to fetch a priest with some holy water and a torch!"

What else could I do against a poltergeist? A condemned poltergeist. A bullbegging poltergeist!

It was a nightmare come true. I dreamt of spirits, but usually the benevolent kinds, not malicious. Granted, this was largely because many evil spirits outside of Horror were taken straight to the Unknown Beyond, and a band of spirits constantly guarded my home to bounce away any unwanted guests. A poltergeist was the worst kind of ghost that could interact with the physical world. Despite all the training from my mom, I never expected to meet one. I specifically tried to avoid the nasty side of the supernatural by working in Noir, Mystery—not Paranormal. Mystery had open correspondence everywhere except Horror and Sci-Fi. I wanted to be a PI partially because I knew that I'd never be sent to Horror.

At least I'd solved the Case of the theater thief. The reports mentioned items as "missing" or "broken." Based on the cameras fuzzing during his tirade and his capability to throw props, I made a safe assumption that the poltergeist was the cause.

I pedaled to the metal back home with my brightest headlights, testing the claims that my car was the fastest in the city. I sped over puddles, hydroplaning a few times. The fear of spinning out was dwarfed by the terrifying memory of that spirit grabbing for my neck.

As soon as I scrambled into the safety of my own home and my usual lights came on, I burst out, "What the horror, guys? You couldn't have warned me? Where were you all?"

My morning glory rustled, and a cool draft waved past me.

"You know what? I don't want to hear it," I said to my unseen friends. "If you think I'm going to sleep after that, you're sorely mistaken. It's only three hours till sunrise, and I have research to do."

I made myself a large cup of hot tea that was loaded with caffeine and sugar, then dusted off a little pocket-book, "Oz's Haunting Survival Book." It was my uncle's guidebook to surviving Horror. For all the times my mom made me read it, I practically had it memorized. Still, I read through it again, looking for every clue to survive a poltergeist Haunting.

"Leave when your only light source in a dark room is a single bald bulb, or lights flicker, or you see the reflection of anyone or anything that's not supposed to be there… Update lights every year, so if they flicker or fuse, you know it's a direct Haunting alert… Never be alone… Never go toward the sound, but don't totally ignore it either. If you must inspect, do so with a friend and a weapon."

The section on Emergency Pack Essentials was one I hadn't bothered with while in Mystery. Now, however, I made a note to search out a church with holy water available. I felt a bit like a Westerner as I strapped on my revolver holster to my belt then added another pouch loaded with matches, a compass, and first aid. Noir had mass printing but no Wi-Fi, so I expected to find paper maps of Shigaqua in any hotel or public service kiosk. I'd grab one later to complete my emergency pack.

With a couple of destinations in mind, I went back to my car. Two more hours and the sun would be up. The dying rain and lifting clouds gave me hope that I'd actually see the sun when it rose.

I drove first to a twenty-four-hour hotel for a map, then to a church to wake a priest and acquire a holy water dispenser. The clouds broke at the horizon to invite the first lightening hues of morning as I went to the library.

I researched everything they had on "tangible spirit" which wasn't much, including their Paranormal history section. I quickly learned that I was correct in calling it a poltergeist. Spirits were rarely tangible in benevolent ways—hence my troubles in finding one to take notes for me. I did a double take when I recognized some names on a particular article. The Case with the most official and substantive commentary on poltergeists included Jonathaniel Mystery's international Case involving the Horror emigrant, Pansy Finster.

With that in mind, I had a phone call to make.

Home again, I poured another tea cup of a less potent flavor and checked the time. It was probably late enough. Despite being two countries apart, Noir was near the same longitude as Margen, Fairy, Fantasy, which meant my family was in the same time zone. It was one more perk about being in Noir that I hoped to enjoy on a long-term basis.

Unfortunately, Margen didn't even have rotary-dial telephones as Noir did. I could only call my parents between the hours of eight and ten in the morning—the time they designated for carrying around their glowing communication orbs.

I dialed the number of the woman mentioned in the poltergeist commentary, formerly known as Pansy Finster. Now, she was known as Marchioness Pansy Fromm, The Unsettled, of Margen. When she answered with her glow ball, I used the name I'd always given her, "Mom."

I couldn't hide the fact that I was a native of Fantasy with half Horror blood. People knew that by judging my dark skin color, crisp and hushed accents, and magical ability. Being an immigrant was one thing that already separated me from regular Mysteries. But being a cousin (once removed) to the bullbegging King of Fairy was another thing entirely. Fantastics knew me as Earl Aeron Fromm, the Haunted, of Margen. It didn't matter if I left my homeland or abdicated my inheritance of half of the kingdom. People didn't know how to act around royalty. It was hard enough already for me to make friends among the living.

So, as soon as I started school in Mystery, I changed my last name to Spade. Only a few people (PI Baldi and Truth Locke included) knew my real name and every title that came with it.

"Aeron?" my mom said over the phone. "It's early. Are you okay?" She sounded tired. She'd always been a late riser.

"Sorry," I said. "I couldn't sleep last night, and I found myself researching your poltergeist Hauntings with Jonathaniel Mystery. Can you tell me about them?"

She didn't respond right away. Then, "You couldn't sleep? But you love sleeping. Why were you researching poltergeists? Are you sure you're okay, Aeron?"

"I'm fine," I lied, and subconsciously fidgeted with my bracelet. "It's just a Case I'm working on with the spirits."

"With a poltergeist?" she nearly shouted. "And how is it with the spirits if you couldn't sleep last night? Aeron, if you don't tell me what's going on, by the Supernaturals, I will—"

"It's fine, Mom," I said. Curses, she was almost as perceptive as a detective, but twice as paranoid. Growing up in Horror did that to people. "And isn't that one of your rules? Don't ask others about their Hauntings unless you want to become involved?"

There was no "nearly" about her shout this time. "Are you involved in a Haunting?"

"No—I don't know. That's what I'm trying to figure out!" We were both quiet as I steadied my breath. Curses, I was still shaken from the night and lack of sleep. I wasn't actually involved with the poltergeist. He was simply a resident of my crime scene and a hindrance to my Case. Curses, I didn't have time to become involved with a Haunting.

"All I need," I said, "is information about poltergeists. You've fought them before. How do you neutralize them?"

"Exorcism," she said. "Water first—holy water if you can get it. Then fire. Aeron, are you sure you're—"

"I'm fine, Mom. What else can you tell me?"

"Aeron, please don't try to fight a poltergeist. They're the worst kind of spirits. Just because they're invisible doesn't mean they can't hurt you. Their most dangerous power is to possess someone, but it's also their weakness."

"Weaknesses, yes," I said, grabbing a pen and legal pad. She'd raised me with the knowledge to kill any monstrous Haunting, but I'd never needed to use it before. I wanted a refresher. "Tell me more."

"Don't make me regret this," my mom sighed. "People can become possessed by inviting the spirit into themselves consciously or unconsciously. Consciously, by welcoming it verbally, or unconsciously by losing themselves in drugs, alcohol, or dark malicious thoughts. Whenever they possess someone, any damage you inflict on the host is also done to them. So, one way to kill a poltergeist is to kill its host, but they can easily escape, and then you've killed a normal human."

"Good to know," I said, scrambling to take notes. "What else can they do?"

"Lots of things," she said. "Trip, push, bite, move, or levitate objects. They tend to focus more on people than places."

Interesting. I wrote a reminder to dig deeper into the backgrounds of the actors and crew members of the Regal Theater. "What else?"

"Poltergeists are tricky. Even though they can touch us and become physical, they can still float through walls like any other ghost. They can have powers of telekinesis to move things without touching them. Now, will you tell me what's going on?"

"Sorry, Mom. It's, er, classified."

"Oh? You've been waiting your whole life to use that phrase, haven't you?"

"Maybe. It's about as useful as I expected."

My mom laughed softly. "So, it sounds like you got the job in Noir. Congratulations, Aeron. We're proud of you." Her voice was sincere, though sad. She wanted me to live closer and come home more often, but I had to chase my dreams while they were still within reach.

"Thanks, Mom," I said, again hoping to sound confident regardless of my terms and conditions to truly be hired. "I miss you guys. I'll try to come home as soon as my new job gives me a break. Until then, give Sam some breath-squeezing hugs for me."

"I will," my mom said. "Your sister asks about you every day, so she'll hear about this conversation. Do you have a good team with you? Ask if one of them is a former priest or clergy, especially if you're fighting a poltergeist. With a transporting spell to the edge of Fantasy and plane ride to Shigaqua, I can be there in less than three hours—"

"No, Mom. Please." I cringed at the thought of my *mom* helping me to solve the Case that was supposed to prove my mettle. "I need to handle this myself. I haven't been assigned an official team, but I'm meeting new people." My mind drifted to Nita and her undefinable characteristics. "Actually, I met Truth Locke yesterday. She says that she knew you and Father at Heartford University."

"Truth Locke? Oh! Truth...yeah." My mom's voice faltered as if she wasn't sure what to say about the woman. "I didn't know her as well as Theo did, but she's, um...honest."

I laughed, understanding all too well. Our conversation continued on different topics as I asked about her, the family, and the duchy in general. I read the news to keep up to date on the big events, but I liked to stay in the loop on a personal basis. We talked a bit longer until my yawns kept interrupting. After quick expressions of love, I hung up and considered my next step to solving the Case.

With the sun sprouting from the horizon, I made my way to bed. I had work to do in my sleep. I set my alarm to go off in two and a half hours, then closed my eyes.

After what seemed like fifteen minutes later, beeping woke me. How did the time go so fast? I felt just as tired as before, but some spiritual traitor pushed back my curtains with a wind gust. Sunlight invaded my room like a conqueror.

"Alright, I'm up," I moaned. If I didn't need to research before my scheduled appointment at the prison, I might have taken my studies back to bed. Reality was a nice place, but I didn't care to live there.

I steamed myself a cup of tea as I went about my morning routine—four hours later than my schedule. I stretched, then went for a quick jog around my neighborhood. I waved to passing neighbors, but they ignored me or shied away as usual.

My spiritual friends wanted me to live as long as possible (to be their messenger for as long as possible), so they helped me to keep healthy habits. Voices corrected my posture, whispered encouragement, then straight out shouted at me while I jogged. Nothing spurred a runner like the thought of something dangerous chasing them. My friends made up for their scares by rolling against my muscles while I did static stretches.

"Thanks, guys," I said before stepping away from them and into my bathroom. After a quick shower, I was dressed and ready to go with a bagel in my mouth. Go figure, Mystery had added surprise raisins inside.

Carpooling to the prison, Truth had asked for me to pick her up from the Shigaqua Police Station. Driving to the station took forty minutes in the morning. Hours after the usual work rush, I made it under twenty. Yes, I stayed within the speed limit.

Walking into the hub of law enforcers and detectives, the place was alive with workers. People called to each other down the hallway of offices or met with low voices in briefing rooms, while others strapped on suits and gear for a big bust. I soaked in the energy and grinned. Someday I'd work beside them as a hired investigator like Truth and Nita.

I found Truth standing just outside the interview rooms, eyes closed, hands at her core with only her fingertips touching.

"Hello, Fromm," she said without opening her eyes.

"How can I convince you to use my Mystery name?" I asked.

"I don't believe in aliases. You are who you are, no matter your name."

I grunted again, annoyed by her answer, but seeing no way to persuade her otherwise. "How did you know it was me coming to talk to you?"

"One, we have our appointment, so I was expecting you. Two, I could hear your expensive shoes walking this way, and three, you wear a distinctive cologne that reminds me of a fungus only found in Fantasy. As I said, you are who you are."

"Fine, but I'm not sure Richard was the intended victim of his murder. In your interviews, was there anyone who might have wanted to hurt Richard to frame William Quigley? Or even to kill the career of Director Stephens?"

Truth shook her head with her eyes still closed. "Knowing the Case was already passed around a lot, I didn't hold back my skills. I read everyone we interviewed, and those who interacted with Richard didn't interact with his dad. I did consider the possibility of someone choosing a random actor to kill in order to taint Director Stephens, but the only man who truly benefited from Stephen's early retirement was the new director who simply volunteered for the sake of the theater. After chasing down former cast and crew, and even those spurned from rejections, I'll give you the advice not to waste your time on the former director. It's a dead end."

I smirked. "You're good at what you do, I'll give you that. But did you know the theater is haunted by a poltergeist?"

Truth's eyes snapped open. I expected doubt, fear, or a little astonishment from my claim, but Truth's expression mirrored a kid opening their new favorite birthday present. "Really? I knew the rumors were true that ghosts resided there, but I didn't know a poltergeist was among them. I sensed a feeling of ill omens and maliciousness around the stage, but that's common around murder scenes."

"So," I said, "knowing that, do you have any advice for me?"

"Advice? Sure. If you're being chased by a taxidermist, don't play dead."

"Err," I slurred, "I meant, how does that shift your thoughts of the Case?"

"Oh, that. Why ask me? It's your Case now. Unless you can find the poltergeist's discarded body. I'd love to read his hands."

"I think he's been dead too long for that, but you worked on the Quigley Case the longest and most recently. You know it better than anyone else, and the best investigators simply know the right questions to ask the right people. Based on the poltergeist's capabilities to move objects and fritz out the cameras, I suspect he's the culprit of the thievery. It's possible he witnessed the murder, but I don't want to confront him if I don't need to. So, tell me, what else do I need to know about the Regal Theater? Is the theater a key factor to the Case or another dead end as a convenient place to kill someone?"

Truth rubbed her palm in thought. "You're expected to examine the crime scene thoroughly. This is Noir, not Paranormal. Poltergeists don't belong here or anywhere outside of Horror and Paranormal states. If you need to work around a poltergeist, you'll need to pacify it. That starts with learning how it got here and why it chose to stay."

I grunted. Pacifying a poltergeist sounded as possible as taming a tornado. Maybe it was possible, but not with the amount of time I had. Narrowing on her last statement, I asked, "Why would the poltergeist leave?"

"Because outside of Horror and Paranormal, Hauntings like poltergeists are weakened," Truth explained. "But you said it witnessed Richard's murder? As the current leading investigator, it's your duty to interview every witness. The real question is, how will you get its honest testimony? Malicious spirits often lie and deceive in seances, but if you can connect with them—find a way to understand them—people are more likely to be honest. Thus, your next problem and my advice: discover who it is and why it's here instead of Paranormal."

Great. I didn't have time to dig into the past of a malicious spirit. I had to search for an alternative. Maybe my interview with Mr. Quigley would provide a better clue.

As casually as possible, I asked about Nita, then hid my disappointment when Truth said that Nita wouldn't join us for our prison visit.

"Is she busy on the Case finding and catching Sponsor?"

Truth nodded. "She's currently undercover as a weapons dealer."

"That's great!"

"I'm afraid I can't say more than that, but it means I had to postpone our trip to the prison for another hour. Can you occupy yourself until then?"

"Sure," I said. "City Hall's down the block. Who can I bug at the personal records center about information on the Quigleys?"

She nodded toward the front windows and the colonial-style building of civil offices. "Ask for Nancy Peters. She knows everything back there."

I thanked her and took a stroll across the street. I'd visited Spyglass's Personal Records Center multiple times while researching Cases at University, but had yet to visit Shigaqua's. As soon as I stepped inside the main room, I experienced déjà vu. I had been there as a spirit with Lestrade two nights ago.

That probably meant that I was on the right track.

The records center was like a library of every boring paper ever written. Instead of stories and histories, the place was full of with ledgers and a backroom of filing cabinets lining the walls and around corners to deeper depths. Nancy Peters turned out to be a woman on the edge of retirement with an overall sagging appearance in a floral dress.

"Who asked for me?"

"Someone who needs the best of the best," I said. She didn't seem in the cheeriest of moods, so I graced her with a friendly smile with a side of pitiful humility that asked for help. "I heard that if I wanted a job done right, I needed to ask for Nancy Peters."

She blinked at my flattery and softened slightly. "What's the job? I don't have a lot of time."

"Of course, I'd hate to waste your time. If you could just point me in the right direction, I can get it myself—"

"What do you need?"

I showed my deep gratitude with another smile. "William and Barbara Quigley of 733 Crooked Road, apartment 1435. Anything you have on them, their family, parents and grandparents as far back as you can give me, if you have it."

She scoffed. "If I have it? Don't ask for the best, then doubt my capabilities. Someone asked for similar information only last month."

"Oh?" I asked. "I'm guessing that was Truth Locke."

"It was that weird gypsy investigator who thinks she knows everything about me."

"Yep. That would be Truth." No doubt researching for the Case when it was her turn. Nancy disappeared between the cabinets for a few minutes before returning with a three-inch stack of files and folders.

Good thing I learned how to research at university. Somewhere in there, I hoped to find a suspect connected to the Quigleys.

I wanted to ask her to research the poltergeist, but I couldn't remember his name, only his face snarling at me with hate. Someone else must have told me his name…right? Even if I remembered, I didn't have a last name or estimated lifetime to narrow the search.

Mrs. Peters gestured at the stack of folders. "Here is everything we have about Mr. and Mrs. Quigley. Where they were born, education, work experiences, even taxes and some financials."

"Thank you, Mrs. Peters. You're a bona fide dame," I said with my most charming of grins. "Do you have anything about other people who've died in the Regal Theater?"

Mrs. Peters blushed with my compliment, but shook her head. "If you give me their names, I can look anyone up, but I don't do locations. You need the county assessment department or the police department for previous Case information."

"Thanks," I said, despite my disappointment. Even if I could remember his name, I wasn't sure there'd be a complete file on him. Poltergeists weren't native to Noir. He had to be from a Paranormal state or Horror zone. Knowing his name and native land were only clues to the real questions: how did he get to the Regal Theater in Noir, what was he doing there, and—if he was involved in Richard's murder—how?

I shook my head to clear it of the poltergeist issue. I didn't have time for a goose chase or red herrings.

CHAPTER 7

A distorted perspective of reality is all too prevalent among detectives, sowing seeds of uncertainty and self-distrust. This may be induced through the cunning manipulations of others, a haze of forgetfulness by imbibing spirits (or spiritual "dreams"), or the forfeiture of consciousness at crucial junctures.

- *Lemuel Gulliver's Travel Guide,*
Vol. 4: Mystery
(with notes by Aeron)

Unlike libraries, I couldn't leave the records center with any files. It would have been impossible to read everything before my evening meeting with Mr. Quigley. At least for any normal person.

I opened the folders to spread the papers and files across a four-seater table to share them with my ghostly friends. Instead of a ghost, a tall and elderly man hunched over my table. Despite the summer warmth, he wore a ragged old coat, scarf, and hat.

"It appears this is merely a one-pipe problem."

I grinned. "Nice disguise, Holmes. It's good to see you again while I'm awake."

He waved a wrinkly hand as if my words were a fly in the air. "Silence, please. Time is of the essence."

Agreeing, I returned to my studies. There was no need to reenact my embarrassing attempt to hug or touch Holmes while he used his manifestation gift. Manifesting took a toll on him in a way I struggled to understand, so he only used his gift for about an hour once every few days. I only had an hour or so with these files, anyway. Time to crack on.

I started with the files on the Quigleys and let Holmes go over the other papers. Anytime he found something of interest or needed a page turned, he pointed urgently.

The Quigleys were fairly run-of-the-mill. Barbara and William had been born and raised in Shigaqua, but far enough apart that they attended different schools. They married a year after graduating and had Richard a year after that. They paid their taxes fully and on time with no suspicious deposits. All paper evidence pointed to Mr. Quigley as an outstanding citizen.

I ran out of time before reading the files more thoroughly. Stacking everything as it was given to me, I thanked Holmes for his assistance and returned the pile to Nancy—who seemed impressed and grateful for my careful stacking. It was always good to befriend those with information. I walked quietly to the doors, then dashed back to the police station. Picking up Truth, I drove with more eagerness than any sane person would toward the prison.

Truth led me through the prison and its many processing steps. They made me surrender my Colt Detective Special revolver and recently-stuffed Hauntings Emergency Pack with its matchbox and stakes. Truth relinquished a Browning Hi Power pistol, a set of cuffs, and a bunch of jewelry I never would have suspected as hazardous. I wished Nita had joined us, but we were already pushing the allowances by asking for two visitors for the same convict at the same time.

We stepped into the visitor's room, guarded inside and outside. Mr. William Quigley stepped into the room, escorted by yet another guard.

Like most men in Noir, William was a few inches shorter than my five-foot-eleven. The picture of him and Mrs. Quigley as teenagers at the playhouse had shown him to be a medium-build of toned muscle. Now, he was a medium build with his stomach poking through the doorway to heavy-set. His head was covered thickly with black hair, salted heavily with grays. He wore a suit of thick black and white stripes and cuffs around his wrists. At least he wasn't considered dangerous enough to add chains down and around his ankles.

More importantly, I studied his face as he walked in, his lips thin with nerves and maybe a little annoyance. His flat eyes and eyebrows shaded between suspicion at new faces (AKA: me) and hope at Truth. As far as he knew, she was the one who'd get him out of there.

"Who's this?" he asked Truth, gesturing to me with his chin.

"Aeron Fromm," she said, slipping with my birth name again. "He's a Fantasy—"

"Investigator," I said, before she could reveal more about me. Curse her and her blabber mouth. Did she have no concept of personal information? "Please, call me Spade. I've been assigned your Case to find the true cause of your son's death."

Mr. Quigley frowned. "I thought that was your job?" he asked Truth.

"Fromm will be your new handler," she said. "He may be young, but his resources go way back."

I sat at the metal picnic bench and motioned for him to do the same.

"So," he said, swinging his legs around the bench. "You're finally gonna solve my son's murder?"

"Yes," I said.

Mr. Quigley scoffed. "The other investigators gave empty promises that they'd do the best they could, then they passed me along to someone else. My trial's next Monday. What makes you think you can solve my Case in five days when others gave up after months?"

"It's only Wednesday. As Ms. Locke said, I have resources and contacts that no one else has."

Mr. Quigley snorted. "You sound like the Sponsor."

I smirked. "Not those kinds of resources. Mr. Quigley. Can you tell me what happened the day of your son's death?"

He groaned, annoyed. "Didn't you read the report?"

"The report that stated your guilt? Sure. But I've been asked to look at every angle."

The convicted man sighed and slumped in his seat. "It started off like any other Friday. I woke up early and drove off to the studio for a short day of shooting. Barbara did her usual routine to get Ricky out of bed. He doesn't eat breakfast, too busy sleeping in. With school out, Ricky lounged around, watching the television, and Barbara cleaned. She works at the laundromat in the late evenings now that Ricky's out of school and she can spend mornings with him. Her job was the reason I had to take Ricky to the theater that night. They normally rehearse on Saturdays, but with the opening show coming up, they were doing a dress rehearsal the night before. I dropped him off, then drove home. I got blamed for his murder just because no one saw me leave or arrive home."

Truth coughed a little. "William, if you don't tell him, I will."

He narrowed his eyes at her. "Tell him what? And how many times have I asked you to call me Bill?"

"Tell him that your and Richard's palms conflicted. You took pride in your part with the theater, but Richard had little care for the extracurricular activity. You argued about his attitude in the playhouse."

William rolled his eyes. "Yeah. The argument that apparently everyone overheard and used as 'proof' to call me a murderer."

"Mr. Quigley," I said, "can you recount the argument for me to the best of your capabilities?"

He groaned. "Normally, I forget our arguments. We had them almost every day. But those were my last words to my boy. I hate the thought that he died thinking I was disappointed in him."

I filed away a mental thought to tell Richard otherwise when I contacted him.

"I tried to tell him what the theater meant to me, but he didn't care. We got into a little scuffle, and he tore off my button—by the door, not up on the catwalk like the police said. It made me furious, but I came to my senses of the scene we were creating, and I left. I expected to resolve our argument at home later that day. I never expected…"

He dropped his head into his hands to hide his sobs. The man seemed genuine, but with his acting career, I had to wonder about his skills to put on a façade.

"Mr. Quigley, who would you suspect of killing your son?"

"I don't know." He shrugged, his expression slipping between despair and rage. "He died there, and it wasn't my fault, but I kind of feel like it is. He didn't want to be there. Ricky only did theater because I thought he should. The theater gave me friends, confidence, and teamwork experience. I hoped it would do the same for Ricky. It lets kids act like kings and pretend to do things they're too afraid to do in real life. I bet it was one of the cast members. They were jealous of my boy for something, I don't know what—but one of them had to have done it!"

His sudden passionate accusation surprised me. Then again, four days before his trial, he was probably desperate for anyone else to take the blame. Witch trials and all that.

"I'll look into it," I said. "Mr. Quigley, is there anyone who might have a vendetta against you specifically?" Yes, Truth told me it was a dead end, but I had to ask. William gave me some names of fellow cast and crew members, including Director Stephens. With each one, Truth gave a subtle shake of her head to add her opinion of their innocence. Trying another lead, I asked. "Do you know anything about the Regal Ghost?"

Mr. Quigley froze and his face tinted white. "No. What ghost?"

Truth squinted and tilted her head sideways. "William," she said, "you know better than to lie to me."

He swallowed heavily and grumbled, "Er, well, almost every theater's said to be a little haunted. There were always stories. Like I said, theaters encourage kids to play pretend, but I never had any personal experiences with any ghost."

"Do you believe in ghosts?" I asked.

He frowned, almost in a defensive manner. "No. Maybe weird stuff happens in Paranormal, but this is Noir. When you're dead, you're dead. What's any of that got to do with my son's murder?"

I smirked. "Yes, but I can assure you, Mr. Quigley, the dead are very much alive. In their own way."

He scoffed. "I swear, every investigator passes me off to a crazier nutter. Honestly, I don't care how you do it. Just give my son justice, and get me outta here."

The guards stepped in, signaling our visitation time ending. Mr. Quigley stood and shuffled toward the door.

As he was ushered out, I asked, "Mr. Quigley, you said you don't want your son to think you're disappointed in him. If you could say anything else to your son, what would it be?"

His mouth and eyes turned sad. "I'd tell him I won't stop looking for the truth of what happened, no matter how much it costs."

Far too soon, it was time to drive back to the theater for my second night.

My dread deepened with every block closer to the playhouse. What was I going to do? I couldn't sleep inside again with the poltergeist raging about. I had an ability that let me talk with the dead, but that didn't make me immortal. I was as human and fragile as any other mortal. Even if the poltergeist was somehow weaker in Noir, he'd had enough power to grip my neck. I shuddered to remember the strength of his hands around my throat.

I briefly wondered if I could convince Mrs. Quigley to let me sleep on her couch. Their apartment was only a few blocks away. No, not likely. Desperate as she was to have her son's murder solved, she was also a woman living alone and unlikely to allow a strange man to stay the night.

Before the sun set, I ran in to make plans with the head of security. Thankfully, it was a different guard this night. He thought I was crazy, and I couldn't blame him, but the guard from the other night probably wouldn't welcome me a second time.

Driving around the theater to the block behind, I spotted two houses on Memory Lane. The one closer to the theater had wood nailed over the windows and a long faded sign posting its condemnation. Making a last second decision, I turned onto its driveway and parked my car. My driver's seat wasn't built for leaning back, so I rotated to sprawl across the entire bench. Funny how comfortable a car could seem when you needed to be awake, but as soon as you tried to sleep in it, it became as comfortable as a stone. The situation wasn't ideal, but anything was better than sleeping in a location claimed by a poltergeist.

I set an early alarm for myself, then measured my breathing and went through my relaxation exercises. Despite my discomfort, I was asleep and drifting from my body within two and a half hours.

The sun was well set, leaving me to see with my ghostly vision under the stars and quarter moon. While my body lay across the car seats, I sat up, not surprised to find a spirit bent over with his head absorbed through the hood.

"Good night, Morse," I called.

The spirit stood with the posture of a gentleman. "Your car could use a tune-up; it's about that time."

I smirked. "Thanks. I'll try to remember when I wake up. Do you know anything about spirits lingering around here?"

"There's a solitary maid in the house ahead. She keeps peeking through the windows at us. She seems rather eager."

"Thanks," I said. "I think we passed a pub advertising its quality ale on the way here if you wanted to check it out."

"I could certainly use the smell of a drink about now," he said, then floated off.

I smiled and turned my attention to the condemned house before me. Wandering into an abandoned home as a normal human would have broken a hundred different rules of Horror survival, but as a ghost, I surged ahead. My career depended on this Case. I needed more information on the murder scene and poltergeist. That meant talking to the neighbors.

I drifted to the desolate house in front of me. Knocking on doors didn't work as spirits, so I gave a customary courtesy clap before entering the private dwelling.

"Hello?" a woman's voice asked. A nervous face peeped around the corner with long silvery hair streaming behind. She gasped when she saw me and came forward eagerly. "Tarnation! 'Tis you? The Haunted Investigator?"

I blinked with surprised eyes. "You know of me?"

"I…yes." She curtsied low. "Word has spread about your coming to Shigaqua, Ace of Spades. You are the living one who visits the dead while he sleeps, are you not? How may I aid you?"

I didn't answer right away, so stunned was I from her awareness and beauty. Her short hair curled around her face with locks of silver. Her every feature was round, from her silver-blue eyes to her bubbled cheeks and full lips.

Spirits in general were more beautiful than their living versions. Wrinkles eroded, hair grew as desired, and scars faded unless the spirit chose to have them (which some did as testimonies of their Adventures). They rarely chose to appear older than their death day, rather, most spirits appeared in their mid twenties or thirties, reflecting their favorite years of life. This spirit was barely a woman, as if she was only a year or two younger than I was. Either she'd reveled in her youth or had died young.

She kept a blotched scar that poked above the low and wide neckline of a fancy hip-hugging dress, though it was her only blemish. The scar invited eyes to her youthful but well-developed left breast. She pinched back a smile and ducked her head from my staring.

I collected myself. "I find myself at a disadvantage. You know my name, yet I do not know yours."

She shrank a little with wide eyes, like a child caught with the last biscuit.

"Norris," she said with another curtsy. "Miss Margaret Norris at your service, Mr. Spade."

"If you don't mind me asking, Ms. Norris, I have a few questions about your neighbors."

She blustered with anticipation. "Yes, Mr. Spade. Anything."

I suppressed my smile and raised eyebrows. She was definitely an eager one. Almost…star struck. I sometimes received such reactions in Fairy, but rarely in Mystery. "Alright, how well do you know the occupants at the Regal Theater?"

"The Regal Theater?" she asked. "Around the block? Oh, they set up entertainment for others, but I find the crowds overwhelming, Mr. Spade."

"Do you know of the poltergeist?" I asked.

Ms. Norris tilted her head. "You mean Neil Martin? The one dressed as the Ghost of King Hamlet?"

Neil Martin. Great. A name like that could be from any era or even genre. His costume as a Hamlet character didn't help age him. When had he lived and died? Where did he come from? And what did he know about Richard's death?

Ms. Norris shrugged. "I met him a few times. He is…a cynical soul. He'd find something to moan about even in Heaven."

An accurate description for a poltergeist. "What about Richard Quigley? Did you meet him before he left the theater?"

She shook her head. "You mean the young lad who died recently on center stage? There was a lot of talk of him, but I never met him, Mr. Spade. I have only attended the closing night performances, and it seemed that the lad had moved on by then. I suspect he may have lingered for the opening night, though it was said that he detested the place."

"As far as I've heard, that seems to be the case," I said. "Unsolved murder victims rarely go directly to the Unknown Beyond, so it's possible he linked himself to his parents or even to his killer to haunt him."

"Oh!" the young woman cried out, smiling. "I may check for you! I mean, I could find him for you. I have a gift of awareness for people around me. If you have his full name, I will find him on the double."

"Thank you," I said, again, astonished by her eagerness. "His name is Richard Quigley. Would you be able to bring him here to me? I have some questions for him about his murder. Hopefully solving it will allow him to rest more fully in peace. His dad, William Quigley, is currently in prison; I don't know which cell. His mom should be easier to find. Barbara Quigley lives in an apartment building not far from here." I gave her the address and directions to the mom's apartment. If Richard was linked to his mom, Ms. Norris would find him. "Would you mind if I wandered around a bit while I waited?"

"No, not at all, Mr. Spade," she blustered. "Please excuse the mess. I haven't been able to clean ever since I died."

I laughed a little and waved her worries away. Even if some spirits could leave footprints in the dust, it was a far cry from the capability to clean.

She closed her eyes thoughtfully, then zipped away through the wall.

CHAPTER 8

Take heed, for the femme fatale, with her treacherous wiles, demands caution. (So...*beware of women? Too late.*)

> – *Lemuel Gulliver's Travel Guide,*
> *Vol. 4: Mystery*
> (with notes by Aeron)

With little else to do while I waited for Ms. Margaret Norris's return, I analyzed her home, hoping to better understand the beautiful spirit.

Despite the dust, bugs, decay, and stuffy air, the house was relatively clean. The couch in the front room was among the last of the furniture, left behind for its bulky size and ripped cushions. In the kitchen, the only appliance was an old stove that would probably cause a house fire if turned on. The walls sagged a little under the weight of the roof and buffeting winds. The wooden planks warped from years of morning dew. Overall, the house was worn, but its sturdy craftsmanship helped it grow this old, and it would probably stand this way for another few decades. Unless the living decided to renovate.

What did that say of Margaret, who chose to be linked to this place?

She had a spiritual gift of awareness for other people? Interesting. That gift was usually given to social butterflies, yet she called the theater "overwhelming." She remained in this abandoned home, all alone, when she could visit the theater with other spirits, despite the spiteful poltergeist.

She appeared in the front room again with her hand inside a spirit, effectively dragging him along. He was sixteen and mostly took after his dad with his flat facial features.

"Hello, Richard Quigley," I said. "My name is Aer—"

"Yeah, yeah, your girlfriend told me all about ya," the boy snapped, "and I saw you questioning my ma. At least you picked up my nudge to ask her about that stupid theater."

While I stared wide-eyed, realizing he'd been the one to prompt my interview question, Ms. Norris stared wide-eyed with embarrassment. "I made no claims to be his girlfriend!"

"Coulda fooled me, the way you prattled on about the 'privilege of meeting the one an' only—'"

"Mr. Spade," she rushed in nervously, "you had questions for this blathering idiot?"

"Hey, I ain't no idiot. What d'ya want? Why'd ya take me from my ma to this clammy place?"

I schooled my expressions as their exchange made me want to laugh, blush, and scowl. "I want to solve your murder."

"Hah!" Richard barked without humor. "Why? I'm already dead. Nothing you do's gonna change that."

"Don't you want justice?" I asked.

"I wanna be left alone. You think I don't know what people've said about me now that I'm dead? The only people who actually cried for me only did it out of fear of becoming suspects. Except my ma. Everybody needs to just leave her alone too. That's why I gave you the info about the stupid theater. You were barking up the wrong tree by questioning my ma like that. She had nothing to do with it. But as long as my murder goes unsolved, all my enemies live in fear of being called out as my killer. That's good enough for me."

"Even your father?" I asked.

"Especially my old man." Richard sneered. "He says he loved me, but all he ever did was tell me to do things I didn't wanna do. I'm glad he got blamed."

"Then you know who killed you?" I asked.

The boy scoffed. "Not really. That was the dumbest part of it all. I was knocked off by a complete stranger."

"What did they look like?"

"Dead."

"Pardon?"

"See, what's the point of try'na get justice when my murderer is already dead? There's no fun in that."

Then the poltergeist was the killer? So much for being "weakened" outside of Paranormal. "If your murderer was dead, how did he kill you?"

The boy shrugged. "Wasn't there a report? Seriously, what kinda amateurs did they give me? My ma's paying top dollar to get my good-for-nothing pa outta jail."

"I'd like to hear your side of the story," I said. "What happened at the theater that day?"

The young man sighed dramatically. "My ma usually dropped me off at the theater for practice, but the dress rehearsal was at a weird time, so my old man had to take me. Going to the theater, we got in our usual argument. That stupid theater was his dream, not mine. He tossed loads of money into that dump of a place. We coulda lived in a nicer place or at least got one of them ritzy transistor radios that I could walk around with, but no! He had to give our money all away to the theater!"

"I can see why you argued," I said, careful with my wording and tone not to portray my opinion of his pride. "So, your father dropped you off at the theater. Then what?"

"He followed me inside, and I wanted everyone to know what I thought of the stupid place. We got into a tiffy, and I snagged his button. He got real mad at that point, calling me by my full name and everything. But then we heard someone laughing on the stage. They sounded looney, you know? Like they'd just won the lottery and were gonna burn every last green in front of some homeless people. It was creepy, like they were taunting us. Pa got spooked and left, saying, 'This conversation isn't over.' I thought about thanking the loon for shutting the old man up, but they just kept on laughing. I followed the voice up the catwalk, called out the chicken to show his face, then something pushed me off the catwalk. I knew I was alone up there—no one had followed me. It was only after I died that I saw his face. And he was pissed."

Confirmation. He'd been pushed to his death by the poltergeist. That kind of testimony would have been solid gold to put a murderer away for life. But Richard couldn't give his testimony to the living. Even if he could, the murderer was dead, and I had no proof. Also, what was his motive? "Did he say anything to you when you saw him?"

"He swore like his waiter brought him fake booze. Like he had any reason to be annoyed. I was the victim! He killed me! But he scoffed and said, 'Better than nothing.' Then he took off. Looney, right?"

Better than nothing? Richard's death was better than nothing? Then killing Richard hadn't been Neil Martin's real goal. If a boy's death was "better than nothing," my stomach churned to think of what worse atrocities the poltergeist might desire.

The conversation gave me a lot to consider.

"Thank you," I said. "Is there anything else you can tell me to bring your murderer to justice?"

The boy frowned. "Just that, from what I hear, that loon still loiters around in the playhouse. Maybe he belongs there like my good-for-nothing pa. But, naw, I don't even care what happens to them. Just see my ma's taken care of, you know?"

"I'll do what I can. Thanks again. You may leave, but before you go, your father wants you to know that he loves you, and will do anything he can to find justice for you."

The young man scoffed one last time before disappearing through the walls. Ms. Norris crossed herself. "God forbid him from receiving true happiness. I sense t'would mean pain to others who aren't deserving of it."

I smirked. "Thank you for bringing him. It wasn't a conversation I'd be happy to repeat, but it was very helpful."

Ms. Norris bowed her head to bite her lip and hide her shy smile from my attention.

"Now, if you don't mind," I said, tilting my head, "I have some questions for you. First, how well do you know me?"

Her shy smile deepened into guilt. "Oh, I've, um, researched—or, I mean, there have been rumors of you, Mr. Spade, and I've, um, kept track."

"You are aware then, that I'm still living?"

"Yes, Mr. Spade. You discovered your ability in Horror when you were five years old and have served the spirits of Fantasy and Mystery every night since then."

I raised an eyebrow. She knew about my childhood incident in Horror?

She bit her bottom lip and shrank. If blood still flowed through her, I had the sense she'd be blushing. "Not everyone knows of you as well as I do. You are an inspiring hero, Mr. Spade, a speaker for the spirits."

"I wonder then," I said carefully, "if I might ask a favor of you?"

"Anything, Mr. Spade," she said eagerly.

"With a poltergeist in residency, it's unsafe for my body to sleep at the Regal Theater while I confront him. May I stay here instead? It would only be for a night or two while I'm on this Case."

"Of course, Mr. Spade! I-I'm unable to clean or make a proper presentation of this house, but t'would be an honor!"

"Thank you."

I was already three days through my week, though now that I had confirmation of the killer, I allowed myself to relax. Thinking of my next task to confront the poltergeist, I much rather preferred to spend my time acquainting myself with this beautiful spirit. I floated to the broken couch and sat with a casual lean as if comfort made a difference to spirits.

"You speak with eloquence," I said, "yet live in this hovel? Either you've been dead for centuries or haven't always lived here. Having spent time in the contemporary Procedural, I'd like to speak plainly with you. Tell me your story."

"As you wish, Mr. Spade—"

"Margaret," I cut her off. "That includes calling me Aeron."

A small gasp escaped her lips before she bit them back. That didn't keep their corners from rising with her bubbled cheeks. She was adorable, yet beautiful all at once.

"As you wish…Aeron." Her shy eyes met mine for a brief moment. Too brief. Then she began, "'Twas the turn of the last century when I was born. I grew up through the Thriller Wars."

Curses, this young woman lived in the days of my great-grandfather. Back then, Mystery had covered the entire northern half of the continent, but as Fantasy's adventurers spread abroad, Mystery civilians caught new Cases with a need for action. Through far too much bloodshed, Thriller became its own little republic. The fighting settled for a time—a dark and depressing time that even impacted Western with dust storms—until a second war began. This time, every continent was impacted as detectives were pulled away from their local issues and into the global espionage of Thriller. Romance supplied soldiers, prisoners of war were sent to Horror, and even Children's was threatened with bombings until Thriller became a substantial territory in Novel.

Yet Ms. Margaret Norris sat before me, seemingly innocent and unscarred from the past.

A lock of her hair slipped in front of her face, and I yearned to push it back. Instead, I watched her lovely neck twist and stretch as she slipped the strands behind her ear. "My papa was a graveyard digger, and my mama was a nurse. The wars kept them both very busy. They were hard times, though we grew strong from them."

She paused in her story and seemed content to leave it at that. That left me confused.

"What about your Cases?"

She chanced another glance at me and bit her lip. When she released her lip, it vibrated as if to cry. Startled, I stood and approached to console her. Oh, wait…how? It wasn't like I could rest a hand on her arm.

"When I turned twelve," she said, "Papa took me on a trip to find buried treasure. Something about a clue left behind from one of his burials. We became caught up in a skirmish between detectives and moonshiners. I was too scared to fight for the lost gold. I disappointed my papa and vowed never to go on another Case."

Despite the awful ending, I smirked. Life was too ironic to allow a vow like that to last. "So then what?"

She blinked at me. "Then I came back here, and here I stayed. My Cases were minor and inconsequential, searching for lost cash in the house, detecting the true answers behind homework assignments, and sneaking peeks of the cute boys in the neighborhood."

She shrugged, sheepish and adorable, while I struggled not to gape.

A life without Cases? I wouldn't have thought it possible to avoid the natural laws of Novel. After reaching the age of twelve, every citizen faced annual conflicts according to their land. Whether they were the victim or villain, sidekick or minion, Cases (official or unofficial) were unavoidable in Mystery. She'd trapped herself inside to avoid the constant need to know the who, what, when, where, why, and how of life?

"What about your own death?" I asked. "Your appearance and scar suggest that you were murdered at a young age."

"Oh, this?" She lightly gestured to the blemish on her chest. "'Tis no more than a birthmark. I like to pretend 'tis a gruesome wound from a mighty battle, though I died after my high school graduation from an awful case of influenza. No harm, no foul."

I stared, astonished. This beautiful spirit had the most boring of lives. It tore my heart apart. Yet I realized something while analyzing her fancy dress and choice to keep her pretend wound. "You may not have had Cases, but you took daydreams to Fantasy for Adventures."

She briefly bit her lip again. "I may be a poet at heart, and I read a lot of Fantasy histories in my life. I admit to venturing on many Cases and Adventures in the safety of my mind. At least I could control those to have happy endings. I…" She hesitated to bite again, harder. "I heard about you on the wind. A living man who could enter the spirit realm. Heir to a Fantasy duchy, no less. I imagined you to be handsome and sought out pictures. They hardly even compare—I mean, your physical self and spirit—" She glanced at me, and it was my turn to pinch back an embarrassed blush. "I hardly imagined you as… I suppose the pictures were outdated."

I cleared my throat and found myself embarrassed, flattered, and unable to meet her silvery eyes.

"Enough about me." She smiled nervously. "Will you tell me more about you?"

"You mean you don't already know everything from the rumors?"

"Oh, I know what they say." She shrugged. "I already know about your past girlfriends and mystical Case solving. Please, tell me, do you plan to catch and detain Sponsor?"

I chuckled. "That would be the dream. Do you know anything about him that might help the Case?"

She shook her head. "Unfortunately, in order for me to use my gift of awareness, I must know their full name."

I frowned. "Surely, someone must know who he is. I thought there weren't any secrets among the dead."

She raised a delicate hand to her chin. "If any benevolent spirit knows, it would likely be PI Harry. He was the last to come closest to catching Sponsor before his untimely accident."

"PI Harry," I echoed, "as in the previous Head Investigator of Silent Sleuth Services? Would you be able to locate him?"

"Do you know his first name?"

I grunted. "No. I'll need to look it up and get back to you."

"Very well," she said, hanging her head. "I wish I could be more helpful to you."

"You've been very helpful. Was there anything else you wanted to know?"

She bit her lip and looked at me through her long eyelashes. "Please, would you tell me about your time in Horror?"

I coughed, and Margaret tilted her head at the gesture. Spirits didn't need to breathe, which made coughing unnecessary. "Sorry, habit from life. But, um, wow. You really want to know about that?"

"Forgive me if 'tis not my place to ask." She bowed her head.

I laughed. "You spilled your life story and worry that it's not your place to ask about one incident from my childhood? You're fine. You just caught me off guard."

She dared to raise her eyes to me, silently begging me to answer her question. I returned to the sofa for the comforting sensation of sitting.

"Um," I began, "I don't remember most of it. I mean, I was only five years old."

"What do you remember?" she urged.

I paused to collect my thoughts. "I remember glimpses of being kidnapped, of feeling lost and scared. At first. I remember sleeping a lot, because I preferred my time with the spirits over reality. What I remember the most was the fight in the Shadows of the Valley of Death." I remembered the armies of monsters, but most of all, I remembered the living shadow sucking away my life, suffocating me, killing me. I suppressed a shudder from the mere thought.

Instead, I considered my impressions from the stories my parents told me. "My parents and Uncle Dunstan fought hundreds of Hauntings in their attempt to rescue me. They fought and struggled so hard…even though it almost killed them." Despite all their efforts, I had still died. The Shadow of the Valley of Death had consumed me. The darkness and terror weren't something I could forget.

"I remember the feeling of dying," I said. "Not of falling asleep and dreaming of my spirit leaving my body, but of truly dying with the pain disappearing and peace welcoming. Then nothing. According to my parents and spirit friends, I did some crazy god-level things in those three minutes of death, but I can only imagine it."

"I'm sorry," Margaret said. Timid and doubting, she reached her hand across to rest on mine. I couldn't feel her touch, though a small impression rested on my mind of how it felt to be touched by a woman's soft hand. She tried an understanding smile, as if she meant the gesture as no more than a condolence. Maybe I read too much into it, but her apprehensiveness said her thoughts were more romantic.

Unsure how to respond, I shrugged. "It was years ago. Besides, having died once lets me relate a little more with my spirit friends." I ended with a grin, hoping to lighten the mood. The return of her timid smile was enough for me. I checked the moon outside to calculate the time. My alarm would wake me at any moment. I stood and flustered to collect myself. More useless habits from life.

"I should get back to work. Thanks for sharing your story." I fumbled for the right words. "After I solve this Case, maybe we can go on a real Adventure or solve the Sponsor Case together."

She looked up at me with hope and wonder. When was the last time this woman felt anything more than regret and loneliness?

I went to the door, but turned back to smile. "I'll be back tomorrow night. Thanks again for letting me stay here."

CHAPTER 9

An annoying BEEP BEEP BEEP woke me at 2:30AM. I really didn't want to wake up. I especially didn't want to wake up to exorcize a poltergeist.

But sleeping across my car seats left a kink in my back and neck. As soon as I convinced myself to move, I reached for my notepad and wrote down my thoughts. I remained in the same position and closed my eyes to better remember.

"Victim identified the poltergeist as the murderer. Name: Neil Martin," I wrote. I couldn't remember exactly what he'd said, but ideas came through. "Better than nothing. What's Neil Martin's end goal?"

Any other information about the night was obscured by the memory of talking to a lovely spirit with silver eyes and a well-placed birthmark.

The temptation to return to sleep grew stronger.

No. My career was on the line. I needed to solve this Case. Just because I had the murderer confirmed by the victim didn't mean I had proof.

I probably should have asked someone for help against the poltergeist, but who would come? Despite my mom being the most willing and qualified person to aid me, she wouldn't help me prove my caliber to Baldi. Most Mysteries feared anything from Horror as much as the next person. While most fears were founded on knowing too little about the subject, I feared Horror because I knew too much about it. It was half of my heritage. It was where I was taken when kidnapped as a child. I never planned to return, and I never expected to face it in Noir, Mystery.

Grabbing tools from my car, I armed myself like I was going to war. Maybe I was overreacting. Maybe I wasn't. Considering the information from my mom, however, I wasn't about to gamble on underestimating this Haunting.

Wearing Mystery clothes had always felt like playing dress up. Trench coats had their uses in Shigaqua's regular rain, and I liked their functional pockets, but felt the need to earn such a uniform. Also, I looked ridiculous in a fedora. Putting on the gear of a Horror felt equally foreign, yet…natural.

Shuffling through a bag I'd packed earlier, I changed into my blackest shirt and jeans that were neither too tight nor too loose. On top of the dark shirt, I wore a light jacket of a bright blue shade—useful to catch the attention from helpers or to be easily slipped off if grabbed. I laced up my running shoes for minimal tripping possibilities and strapped my emergency pack to my belt, across from my holster. I checked all of my weapons and tools, especially my revolver: safety on, loaded with six bullets and spare clips of silver and gold… just in case.

Considering the poltergeist specifically, I packed my matchbox and aspergillum of holy water near the front and top of the pockets. I even left a goodbye note in my car in case I never came back.

I went to the Regal Theater to confront the poltergeist residing there. Please come help if you can. If I don't come back after sunrise, please tell my mom that I'm sorry.

I signed it with my birth name and hoped to return and burn the note before anyone saw it.

The strangest part about going to confront a poltergeist was that I needed to be awake. I had no gifts as a spirit to fight him. Maybe if I had tangibility to hold my aspergillum, or the gift to dispel spirits like Uncle Oz, then I could fight the poltergeist. I was more vulnerable in my body, but I could also do more than talk. So, I took the gamble.

Street lights offered spots of relief between the darkness of Shigaqua's lonely roads. I turned on my flashlight and forced myself through the shadows. Rounding the block to the theater's back alley, faded lights perched high on the walls to define the shadows. Gulping and gripping my flashlight more tightly, I pushed ahead.

Reaching the Regal Theater's back door, my motions alerted the security lights, easing my nerves a little. I opened the door with the spare key given to me from the security earlier and swung the door open wide. Darkness greeted me. The porch light shone only a step or two beyond the door, and my flashlight did little to quell my fears.

My mind no longer stood on that porch, but was lying on an altar with the Shadow of the Valley of Death looming over me.

The darkness would devour me. Again.

It took every ounce of my bravery to remain on the back porch and not to flee back to my car. But that was all. I couldn't force myself to step inside that dark building with only my flashlight and tools. I stood there long enough to be called a coward, staring into the dark, forcing my breathing to slow. My pulse throbbed through my brain, despite my efforts to calm myself.

Sliding my light around the walls, I found the light switches. Yes, turning on the lights would scare away most ghosts who didn't want to accidentally interfere with the mortal state, but I figured the poltergeist wouldn't have those worries.

The switches were only three feet away. I could reach it with one step…one step into the darkness.

A tune came to mind. My mom had taught it to me for moments like this. I hadn't thought of it for many years, but it came back to me as I stood staring into the dark abyss. I hummed it softly. Its emboldening tune encouraged me to take the first step over the threshold. It was more than a step. I leaped into the room to slap the light switches on.

Light. Glorious light.

My heart relaxed to recognize the misshaped shadows as costumes and props. I shuffled through my emergency pack for my holy water dispenser when the back door slammed behind me.

I jumped a foot in the air. Curses! Was the poltergeist behind me?

I put my back to the wall beside the light switches. Yes, the ghost could go through walls, but if it decided to turn off the lights, at least I'd be close enough to turn them on again.

"I'm welcome here," I said, partially to the poltergeist and partially to myself as a confidence booster. "The owners of this theater invited me and gave me access to this location. I am not a trespasser. However, any malignant being who might be here is not welcome, and I invite you to leave."

With the most authoritative voice I could muster between quivering, I said, "By the God of Horror and all His Supernaturals, I command you to return to the pits from whence you came."

I shook my holy water for good measure. Supernaturals, I had no idea what I was doing.

A rogue breeze wafted past my ear with a hint of a chuckle. Curses, he *knew* that I was clueless.

"Hello?" I called. "Where are you? Show yourself!"

The chuckle mocked me again, distant. I turned about, checking for anything that moved. A shadow flickered from my light, and I jerked in that direction. My light reached into the stage area, but found nothing out of place. The singular Ghost Light bathed the stage in an eerie blue light.

Where was the poltergeist?

I held my breath to listen for the faintest movement. Seconds ticked by, then minutes. I barely dared to move, but the tension suffocated me. My eyes grew weary from darting to every wall and corner that was too silent.

The fake walls creaked on the stage, and I sprung toward the noise. The lights from the workshop filtered onto the stage, but the fake walls were specifically placed to keep light from entering the set from behind. The ghost light and my flashlight became my beacons as I searched for the poltergeist's location. My light zipped between the fake walls, waving the shadows around me.

Silence answered me. Was that better or worse than another door slamming?

I hummed my childhood tune again. A floorboard creaked, and my song stuttered. I paused with bated breath, but the silence was stifling.

"I can be brave," I sang. "When the ghosts groan and monsters moan, I can be brave."

Managing another step in the dark silence, I scanned my flashlight across the room. More light switches for the stage were a few steps away.

"When the doors screech and blood suckers leech, I can be brave."

I flipped on the switches, half expecting a specter to greet me. It looked like I was alone. But looks could be deceiving.

"When the wolves cry and I think I might die, I can be brave."

I stepped away, careful to keep my flashlight on and handy in case the poltergeist decided to switch the lights off.

My voice grew stronger with the lights and with each verse. I sang the little tune until even I grew annoyed with it. Perhaps I was pushing the poltergeist back, but I needed to do more than that. I needed to overpower it. I needed something stronger. I switched out my tune for a hymn of fire and power. Maybe if I agitated it enough, it would show itself to make me stop. Then I could properly fight it. If anything, the new gusto kept me awake.

I reviewed possible conversations to have with the poltergeist—as if we could chat over tea and carry a civil interview. I couldn't completely eradicate him yet. I had too many questions for him. I needed to find a way to prove his guilt of murder.

"Neil!" I called through the fully lit stage. "Neil Martin!" Demons rarely ignored the call of their full names.

A tall black curtain waved on stage left. Found him!

"I know it's you," I said. "I know you killed the boy. Why? If he wasn't your ultimate goal, why kill Richard Quigley?"

An angry moan quivered the curtains.

"You're a murderer!" I shouted. "By the authority I hold as a speaker for the dead, I command you to speak! You've been accused of the murder of Richard Quigley! Explain your defense or depart to meet your condemned fate!"

I raised my dispenser to shake it at the curtains when a horrid scream blasted across the stage. I blocked my ears, then covered my head as the overhead lights shattered from the sound.

Screams escaped my own mouth as I ran away from the stage. Wrenching the back door open, I found relief with the sun's light reaching over the skyline. It was early enough for the streetlights to still be on, though I still used my flashlight as I ran for my car and sped home like a coward.

CHAPTER 10

Firearms! Blades! Implements of warfare aplenty!
The denizens of Mystery exhibit a peculiar fondness for
arming themselves. (Solving crime can be dangerous. Keep a
gun and/or blade handy.)

- *Lemuel Gulliver's Travel Guide,*
Vol. 4: Mystery
(with notes by Aeron)

Running was the natural and smart response to an unseen force breaking lights and screaming your ears out. Any other Noir investigator would have done the same thing, right?

At least, that was what I kept telling myself to feel less like a coward.

After a few hours of sleeping in my own bed in my own haunted home, my head was clear enough to reconsider the Case. I needed to rethink it. The poltergeist wasn't going anywhere, and he wouldn't tell me what happened, so I needed to figure it out myself.

I grumbled at my lack of resources while I was awake. I had no partners, no team, and no database. Back to the personal records center then.

Wondering if I could stop by the Silent Sleuth Services to possibly see Nita again, another beautiful thought guilted my heart. Margaret was her name, right? I closed my eyes and tried to picture the lovely spirit, but only remembered the light shades of her eyes and hair, the shape of her face, and a particular scar that invited wandering eyes. All the lessons and lectures from my mom about lust banished that second image from my mind.

I didn't have time for distractions, anyway. I needed to research Neil Martin. Who was he? How had he died? How had he become a poltergeist in Noir, and why had he killed Richard Quigley?

Yes, I had confirmed the murderer from the witness of the victim, but I still had a lot of work to prove it. And only three days to do it.

I didn't make time to exercise before dressing with a light green vest and heading up to Shigaqua's Personal Records Center again. I had to remind myself again about avoiding distractions as lights flashed across the street at the Shigaqua Police Station.

Focus on the Case first. Pulling out my charm for Nancy Peters again, I asked about Neil Martin, throwing in a hint that he probably died at the theater about a century ago.

"Here he is," the wrinkly woman said, passing over the thin file as if it was a treasure beyond worth simply because it was a piece from her archives.

"Thanks. This is everything about him?"

"Everything we have." She gave me a warning look not to doubt her archiving abilities again.

I flipped open the file and found a grainy picture, aged brown. It was him alright. I recognized the poltergeist despite his content smile in the photo. Scanning the information, I found his migration records. He came to Noir from Paranormal. Go figure. Being a native of Paranormal probably gave him the capacity to become a poltergeist.

Hold on, what were his dates? His death date was listed as only seventeen years ago, and he'd been a mere eighteen years old at the time of his death. This was the aged Ghost of King Hamlet? If not for his picture, I might have second guessed Mrs. Peters' records.

With too much on my mind, I turned back to the woman to say, "You're a swell bird, Mrs. Peters. Would it be possible for you to request the rest of his files from Paranormal?"

"Yes," she said with an eyebrow raised. "But you're working the Quigley Case, ain't ya? You'll need those files sooner than the week it usually takes. I can have them expedited by tomorrow, but you'll owe me one."

I thought about it, then shrugged. "As long as you don't ask for anything inhumane, I'll owe you a big one. You're the killer diller of the archives."

She grinned with a hint of mischief, then waved me away.

The files were meager enough to study thoroughly within a half hour, giving me little information and extra time. I wouldn't learn more until his Paranormal files arrived, so I returned my studies to Mrs. Peters and wandered across the street to the Shigaqua Police Station. Indeed, the place swarmed with after-lunch chaos. Some police chief shouted commands to various teams as they geared themselves. Ross, Truth, and Nita stood at attention, receiving instruction from another detective with the name badge: TJ.

"If you pass their little tests and inspection," TJ said, "we expect Sponsor's number one to show. We need to let him believe that he's in control of the situation. Don't be a push-over, stand your ground, but don't push him so hard that he'll push back. His cronies will be watching the area to make sure you're alone, but we'll have men on them. You may be surrounded, but they will be too."

"Yes, sir," Nita said with a curt nod. I smirked. Something about her expression said this wasn't her first undercover operation, but she listened and responded with duty. She was as alluring as mystery itself, wearing a pink shirt and loose red scarf under a black suit jacket with matching trousers and a belt around her waist. A little black cap pinned up her hair.

Focus. Why was I there again?

"What's going on?" I asked Ross, approaching them. "Did you catch the guy from yesterday?"

"No," he growled. "Someone tipped him off, and he was a no-show. But we got a better lead today. Nita's goin' undercover for a weapons deal. We've worked this angle well enough to poke Sponsor's interest. Rumor has it he'll send his number one man to oversee the deal."

"Really? That could be a huge step to catching Sponsor. Do you think you'll make history today?"

"That's the plan," Ross said. "Detective TJ's heading the operation and feels pretty confident we'll get to Sponsor through this lead. You wanna do a ride-along?"

Sheer excitement replaced all thoughts of responsibility. "You bet!"

Nita's attention jerked our way, proving that she'd been listening to our conversation. For some reason, she became tense with Ross's invitation. "What? He can't come. It's a sting—he'll ruin the whole operation."

"I'll stay in the communications van and won't touch anything."

"But he's not a cop or investigator," Nita said. "He's practically a civilian."

Truth snorted. "Hardly. He's actually—"

"It's just a ride-along," I said, cutting off Truth before she told the whole precinct about my heritage. "I'll refrain from making suggestions. You won't even hear any back-seat driving from me."

Nita stood firm even as I followed the rest of the crowd toward the back exit. She eyed me with her stern frown until the moment I passed her.

"Why did you try asking me out?"

I paused to raise an eyebrow and answer her directly. I'd asked for drinks, not a date. "I just wanted to see if we could be friends. But if it developed into something deeper, I wouldn't have complained." I finished with a teasing wink.

Her stoicism cracked with a slow blink that I'd almost call an eye roll. She muttered, "How can you be so naïve and intimidating at the same time? When you're destined to ride off into the sunset on a unicorn with a princess, well, how can any other relationship with you end in any way but heartache?"

My mouth dropped a little from her bluntness, unsure how to argue her statement.

"Well," she continued, folding her arms and staring me down despite her shorter height, "you talk to the dead? Then you can dig up people's pasts or dirty secrets, right? Digger?"

"Hey," I said, finding my defense again, "that's not what I do, and that's not the reason Ross calls me that." At least, I hoped not. Nita's expressions were too incremental to tell if her slight sigh was for relief or disappointment. Either way, "Threats don't create real friends. And that's all I wanted. Not a Romance with a unicorn and a sunset. Just a friend. Is it too much to ask for a friend in this sleazy city?" I finished with my arms spread wide like asking the heavens for a hug.

The only part of her that revealed her curious surprise was her big currently-hazel eyes. With the smallest of head shakes, they turned brown. "No. I suppose it's not too much to ask."

I blinked and tried a light smile. "Does that mean we can grab some coffee after this?"

Her downward stare returned. "Don't even think about leaving the van, Spade."

"I don't make promises during Hauntings," I said automatically, then let my mojo sneak in, "but I'll cross my heart and hope to die if something so terrible happens that forces me to leave the van. The only reason I can think of is if you're endangered in such a way that only I can help you, despite the many police officers ensuring your safety."

Her cheeks shaded pink beneath her continued glare. "Then we should have nothing to worry about."

I joined the back of the radar van with Truth sitting between me and Nita. The drive was long and uneventful as we took extra turns. Many of the cameras were already set up around the area, so I enjoyed sitting in the back with the radar systems.

We parked three blocks away from the site. Truth fiddled with Nita's jacket to conceal her handgun, then sent her off with a simple, "Not like you'll need it, but good luck."

Nita graced her with a tight smile, eyes flickering to me in the middle of it. Then she was taken away in a little sedan to the sting site.

She arrived on time, but stayed in her car as she waited for her contact to come. Sitting in the back, watching the cameras with Truth, the woman gave me no warning.

"Your relationship with death complicates your life."

"Pardon?" I asked, thoroughly confused.

"All your palm lines point to death. Even if you survive this week, you'll have no life if you spend it all with the dead. You might know who you are, but the denial of your heritage makes you just as lost as Nita."

I stared at her, waiting for an explanation. When I asked, she simply shook her head. "You'll find out soon enough… probably."

Residents of Mystery were odd, but this woman was another level of weird.

The perp arrived, and Nita did a five-star act to play him like a fiddle, demonstrating expert-level knowledge of the illegal machine guns. A black limo pulled up, and everyone leaned forward.

Truth leaned almost against the CTV glass to analyze the newcomer. "That must be Sponsor's number one man. Can anyone ID him?"

He stepped out, surveyed the trade, then nodded to his cronies to seal the deal. The cops swooped in. Two minutes later, the man was identified by his driver's license as James Clay.

Truth stood to leave the van.

"Where are you going?" the driver asked.

"Permission to approach the scene, sir? I need to read his palm. His daily activities may give us more information about Sponsor than any of his coerced confessions."

"Stay in the van, Fantasy fr-Fantastic. You're safe here, and we can't compromise the sting. Let the cops do their job."

Truth scowled. "I need to confirm James Clay's identity."

"We got his ID. Sit back and wait your turn. You'll get a chance after he's secured in a cell." After he "accidentally" slipped another ethnic slur, I frowned and stood with Truth.

"The department asked for their help," I argued. "Who are you to deny—"

"Didn't you say there'd be no backseat driving?" he growled at me. Truth and I glared at him together, but obediently sat back. Truth muttered a string of words in another language, too quiet to decipher.

James Clay shouted for his lawyer as he was escorted with his cronies to backseats of police vehicles. The coms were crowded with cheers as Nita joined us in the van again. We headed back to the station, following one cop car behind the convicts.

"You were amazing," I said to Nita. "Where did you learn to use those weapons? I've been trained in more than a few, but—"

Tires screeched ahead as our only warning before our van slammed us against our seatbelts to a sliding stop. The front window showed that we were stuck in a two-lane tunnel. The exits were far enough away to require headlights in the evening light. Our radios crackled with a shout before it fizzled to static.

The ratta-tat-tat of automatic weaponry clattered through the tunnel.

"Get down!" Nita shouted.

We all ducked and slipped out of our seats, covering our heads with our hands as the front window shattered with bullets. Our driver shouted in pain as he crawled into a ball by his seat.

"They're 'rescuing' Sponsor's man," Truth said. She grabbed two walkie-talkies from the van equipment and paired them. "This confirms his importance. Nita, make sure he doesn't get away."

I snapped my Colt Dick Special into my palm and joined Nita at the door.

"What are you doing?" she asked. "This is a ride-along. You stay in the van."

"I can help," I said.

"Don't get shot," Truth said, leaping from the back of the van before anyone could argue further.

Nita groaned, but accepted her walkie-talkie, then followed. There were shooters at the front of the tunnel. Being the last vehicle in the escort, the three of us squatted around the van for our barricade.

Headlights shattered and went dark as bullets broke them. "Shoot," Nita cursed.

I didn't hear her. My mind froze in the sudden coldness of the tunnel. I was swallowed in the shadows. Again. The darkness would kill me. Again.

Vague memories and stories of my childhood bombarded me. Being stolen away from my home. A wicked witch who commanded monsters of Horror. Snakes binding me to a stone altar as a solid shadow…consumed me.

As much as I wanted to tell myself that everything was alright, that the darkness wasn't dangerous, the gunfire didn't ease the situation. Meanwhile, warnings from my uncle Oz's "Haunting Survival Book" echoed back and forth through my mind. "It's never just a power outage." And this wasn't just a power outage. It was an ambush meant to blind us, kill us, and free our best lead to Sponsor.

"Nita," Truth said from somewhere in the black nothingness, "can you tell what's going on?"

I hadn't heard Nita leave us. Either she was incredibly stealthy, or I was too lost in my own mind. Probably both.

"Don't worry about it," Truth said to Nita's unheard response. "Can you locate the shooters? Find a better angle to remove their chaos. Fromm," Truth said. "Hey, Fromm, calm down. Your whimpers will give away our position."

Was I whimpering? Fingers then a palm slid over my arm. Curses, I trembled beneath her touch.

Truth passed a brick-like device into my hand. "Here," she said. "I need to step away to grab a flashlight from the van, but this walkie-talkie's dialed to Nita's frequency. Stay calm, Fromm. I'll find some light."

"No," I spoke with staccato syllables. "Please, don't go. Please. I…I—"

Another round of gunshots shattered the night.

It took everything I had not to scream. I shook like a leaf in the wind. I hated this. I hated that I couldn't stop it. I hated how weak I felt as the fear paralyzed me.

"Fromm, I'll grab a flashlight."

Truth's hand pulled away from mine.

"Wait—take me—"

I sensed her body jerk as Truth yelped beside me.

Curses—curses! Had I killed her because I was too weak to let her go?

She cursed a string of words that sounded like a hex. Gunshots fired close by. Truth muttered more hexes as a metal box rattled across the pavement. A latch opened, then plastic and metal devices rummaged together with her search.

A flashlight clicked on and illuminated our immediate surroundings.

My breath escaped me in sweet relief. Light. I could see again, and my mind slowly returned to normal. I was still in the same place as before. Truth crouched beside me, clutching the flashlight loosely in one hand and a ripped piece of fabric in her other to unsuccessfully staunch the wound on her forearm.

"Let me get that," I said, brain snapping into gear. Finally.

She handed another flashlight to me, which I held between my shoulder and chin as I made quick work of the bandage, just like my mom taught me. Then I pulled out my revolver.

Nita whispered from the walkie-talkie, "Is Truth okay?"

"A bullet grazed her. She'll be alright."

"I made it to a side angle," Nita continued, "but this tunnel's too narrow. I lost sight of James Clay. I still can't get a good shot at the shooters. Where are you guys? What's holding you up?"

"Truth was shot for one thing," I muttered.

Truth cried out as she tried and failed to grasp her pistol. "I can't hold it. I think they got a tendon."

"Shoot," Nita cursed. "Spade, I need you to give me some cover. You don't need to do anything heroic, only get them to move."

I allowed my eyes to blur as I focused on my hearing. The shooters were near the middle of the caravan. Probably in the middle of the tunnel. I tried to remember what I saw of the tunnel before all had gone dark.

Dark.

No, stop. Focus.

"Spade! Make yourself useful and shoot!"

I winced. Never before had I needed to shoot at a living person. I steadied my breathing and convinced my mind that it was just another training session at Spyglass University. No, those were too stressful. I was shooting with my mom as she quoted rules to survive Horror.

"Nita, get down," I said into the walkie-talkie.

"What? Is your aim that bad?"

Truth, on the other hand, responded with a knowing smirk. What did she know? And how did she know it?

Whatever. I rolled my flashlight to the side of the tunnel to shine on the cars ahead. Then, I spun away from the truck, facing down the tunnel and enemies. I fired two shots per second. One. Two. Three. Four.

Silence.

CHAPTER 11

Be it a transient cloud of forgetfulness or an enduring veil
of memory, humanity possesses an unfortunate
proclivity for forgetting essential information.
*(This is more permanent than the earlier comment about
distortive perspectives)*

> \- *Lemuel Gulliver's Travel Guide,*
> *Vol. 4: Mystery*
> (with notes by Aeron)

The realization of what I'd done hit me as if I'd fired at myself. Those were people I shot. The spraying blood had been a deadly confirmation. I'd shot at real living people. Not paper targets. Not Hauntings. Human beings who made a couple of bad decisions that put them on the wrong side of the law… on the wrong side of my gun.

I ducked behind the truck and holstered my revolver with shaking hands.

"Fromm?" Truth asked, concerned. She stood slowly and offered to help me to my feet. I took her offer with a quivering hand. My legs wobbled. I moved too fast and doubled over to lose my lunch.

"Hey," Truth said, petting my back like I was a dog. "What did I tell you? You got past the darkness. Nice shooting."

Why did those words chill me with remembrance? Hadn't she said something similar when we first met? More bile rose from my throat. Had she seen this future through my palms?

"Shoot," Nita cursed quietly in the walkie-talkie. Then she shouted across the tunnel, "Shoot it all! Are you serious, Spade? You held back on us!"

"I never said I couldn't shoot," I said, wiping my mouth, "but I was distracted."

"Your mom taught you?" Truth asked.

I nodded. Most Fantastics, like my father, considered guns to be primitive compared to magics, but my mom was a born and raised Horror. She taught me the uses of gold and silver bullets and how to make each bullet count.

Nita rushed the downed criminals to clear their weapons. Truth joined her to secure their hands, and I slowly stepped beside them. One man moaned loudly as he held his bleeding wrist. Two others breathed heavily, with wounds to the upper chest and thigh. One man was dead, shot in the head because that had been the only visible part of him when I had fired.

Unfortunately, our rescue hadn't come fast enough. There was another body wearing a uniform. A cop knelt beside him, already applying first aid, but from what I knew from my mom's medical training, the situation didn't look hopeful. I flashed my light on the downed cop's badge. Detective TJ.

I hardly knew the man, but his casualty weighed heavily on me. Would I see him as a spirit soon, or would he move on to the Unknown Beyond?

A distant wail of sirens cried into the night. For some, it was a sound that foreshadowed mourning families. For others, it was the only thing that would cry for their departed souls.

I gulped heavily and whispered, "I'm sorry."

"Yeah," Nita muttered, "you should be. You should have shot them sooner. Then, Sponsor's number one wouldn't have escaped, and our people wouldn't have been shot."

I frowned at her, and Truth sighed.

"Better late than never," the older woman said. "Thanks for helping when you did."

Nita scoffed. "But he held out on us when we needed him."

"Sorry," I muttered again. "I've never shot at actual people before. There's…more blood than I expected…" My voice drifted off as I became mesmerized by the growing puddle of red. Why wasn't it stopping?

"Nita," Truth said from somewhere in the fog, "get him out of here."

The young woman huffed, then stood from her work at the dead ambusher. A gentle hand took my shoulder to steer me away from the scene.

"Come on, Spade. Let's go give the cops our statements."

My mind panicked. The hand on my shoulder giving direction, the bodies behind, the sirens ahead and growing closer.

"Curses," I swore, "am I going to jail?"

Nita turned an incredulous face on me, then laughed. I'd never even seen her properly smile before, but she laughed—now, of all times? The happy sound jarred my thoughts and broke my daze a little.

"How can you laugh at a time like this? I just killed a man!"

Her laughter faltered into a patient smile. If I wasn't so frustrated and scared, I might have called it cute.

"Spade," she said, "you were acting with the police in self-defense. There will be paperwork, sure, but you're not going to prison. Truth and I can witness to your cause for offense. Well, here." She handed me a set of Truth's bangle bracelets. When had she taken them? "Try to unhook these. Truth calls it a relaxer charm, but it's really just a colorful mind-eye co-ordination puzzle that helps after experiencing trauma."

Confused but curious, I began to fiddle with the bangles. They were interlocked together, but if Nita said they could be unhooked…

The rainbow of bangles and flashing cop lights of the approaching ambulance played kaleidoscope with my eyes. The urge to run boiled in my stomach and threatened my esophagus again.

Detective Ross spotted us and jogged over. I finally managed to slip the bangles into just the right position to separate them.

Nita leaned over with the hint of an impressed smirk. "You're smarter than I thought. But can you put them back together and do it again?"

I focused on the puzzle while I talked with Ross, detailing everything I remembered (outside of my blackout). My voice felt hollow as I described the shooting, pushing away the images of the bodies and blood from my mind by concentrating on the colorful rings in my hands. Nearing the end, my breathing still quickened and vomit threatened again, but I managed to finish my report without breaking down. Ross gave me a few curious looks, but clapped me on my shoulder with a, "Thanks for your help," then went to question Nita.

Without the aid of the colorful puzzle, she spoke even more impassively than I had. She reported the exact positions of our attackers, us, our movements—even in the dark—then the result. Another cop came to us to confirm our stories. Focusing on the puzzle had a surprisingly calming effect, and I was able to speak with a tiny bit more normalcy. The crime scene eventually swarmed with cops, detectives, and paramedics.

I stared at Truth and Nita in wonderment as a paramedic redressed Truth's arm. They both acted so collected and normal. Maybe one day I could face attackers in the dark without hesitation.

Truth spoke to Nita, nodding toward me. Barring her shoulders like she'd received an assignment, Nita walked toward me. With every other step, her tension eased until she no longer needed to fake a relaxed posture.

"How," I asked, "can you be casual around casualties?"

She blinked. "Well, I don't know. Practice? It's never bothered me for as long as I can remember… Come on, let's get out of here. Didn't you have some place you wanted to take me?"

"What?"

"You invited me to grab some coffee earlier. Let's go."

"What—now? But the crime scene—the people—"

"We've given our reports. Well, Truth can handle the rest. She'll probably enjoy the police visiting her hospital bed, even if it's only to confirm statements. The paramedics think it was a clean shot, but she'll stay the night as a precaution. She'll be fine. Come on, your car's at the police station, right? It's only a five-minute walk back, then we can go wherever. You need to get out of your own mind, and Truth says I should let you buy me a drink, so let's go."

I blinked, unsure how to switch shifts between the shock of gunfire to shock of Nita's impromptu outing. I was unsure if I'd make for pleasant company in my current state, but my intuition said this chance wouldn't come again.

A memory of a beautiful spirit flashed across my mind. I wasn't courting anyone in my sleep, was I? How would that even work? I didn't remember kissing her or offering any promises of exclusivity. I'd only met her last night. Besides, Nita had been the one to invite me (with Truth's urging), and we were only going out for a drink. Maybe dinner too if my appetite returned after losing my lunch.

I managed to stand and hand back the bangles puzzle—all connected. "If you insist."

It still felt odd to walk away from the tunnel. As if I was fleeing the scene of my own crime, guilt ate at me for leaving it behind. The cold night air and brisk walk helped to clear my head a little. We said nothing for the first couple of blocks, walking side by side, stepping farther and farther from the scene of death and terror. With each step, my thoughts cleared, and I made a plan for our outing. It started with an apology.

"Sorry that I wasn't more responsive back there," I said. "I've never shot at actual people before."

"I'm sorry," she said. The cracks in her stoic expression showed that she actually meant it. "Wouldn't it be nice to live in a world where nobody shot at anybody?"

"That would be nice. But then we'd just have more knife fights." Or magical "accidents." My homeland in Fairy didn't need guns to kill people.

Nita snorted with agreement. "I'd rather not think about it anymore."

My turn to agree. "Distracting myself will be difficult, but I have an idea."

"Oh?" A small smile teased her lips.

We reached my car at the parking garage, and I went to open the passenger side door for her.

She took a good look at my personalized roadster. "Fancy."

I smirked with a shrug. As I said, I was both proud and embarrassed to drive the fastest car in the city. "It was a gift from my grandfather." Mostly because it had a lot of 'horse'-power. Unfortunately, that joke only worked if people knew my grandfather was Duke Konrad Fromm, the Horse, of Margen.

"Hey, Morse," I said to the passenger seat. "Make room for Nita."

"Who's Morse?"

"A ghostly friend who likes to ride in my car."

"You can see him?" she asked, blinking and hesitating to sit down.

"No, but he's there often enough that it's a safe assumption. He can't hurt you. The worst he'll do is change the radio frequencies to the opera station."

Nita's tease of a smile almost became true as she buckled herself in. It was a clear night, so I left the convertible top down. When I started the engine, I had the pleasure of watching her eyes go wide from its beastly grumble. I chuckled as she gathered her wits again.

"Where are we going?"

"On an Adventure," I announced like a dramatic narrator.

Nita lifted an eyebrow at me. "Where?"

I laughed. "It's the Fantastic way of saying, 'I don't have a clue where we're going.' I don't really care, as long as it's away from that tunnel. An unplanned outing is like a road trip. Point out anything that looks interesting, and we'll stop there."

Her smile became thin as she searched the road. Was she suddenly feeling shy? Why?

After five minutes of driving through town without any points of interest, I offered, "How about the Deerstalker Club?"

Her eyebrow lifted again. "Swing dancing?"

I grinned. "I've never been, but it's the talk of the town. Shall we check it out?"

Her curious half-shrug seemed to mean, "Sure."

It was a fifteen minute drive to Deerstalker Club, and the whole time I scratched and scrambled to talk about something intriguing. Nope. I was a sweat ball of nerves as if this was my first outing ever, not just my first outing with Nita. I blamed the recent shoot out for my raised anxiety and empty mojo.

Parking, I offered my arm to escort Nita into the brick building with a lit-up sign and big band music blaring from its cracks. Seeing our approach, a bouncer frowned, crossed his arms, and moved to block the doorway.

I gave him my most charming smile. "Is there an entrance fee?"

"Yeah," he grunted. "And you cain't afford it."

Doubtful. "Name the price."

Like my smile, his frown never wavered. "Your ancestry."

I blinked. Did he know who I was? Before I could panic, he continued, "I could let you people in, but you'd make everyone mighty uncomfortable. Go to Harlem Heights, where you belong."

My gut twisted with his mouth. He didn't know who I was or how much money I had, and he didn't care. He denied us access for no other reason than our skin colors. My professors had warned me about this when I told them of my plans to leave Procedural for Noir. Like their technology stuck with record players and dial phones, Noir's society was stuck with a stigma of racism. Nita wasn't as dark as I was, and I wasn't as dark as my mom, but all this bouncer saw was that we weren't peachy like my father.

Nita sided to me, "Do you want me to incapacitate him?"

"No," I said. "He's right. I don't belong anywhere there's discrimination. Not for a fun night, anyway. When serving as an ambassador for my cousin's kingdom, however—" I gave the bouncer a wolfish grin "—shutting down unjust businesses is a different kind of fun."

I turned on my heel and let the bouncer sweat over the mystery of my authority. Nita followed my lead and raised a half smile and eyebrow.

"Can you actually shut down a Mystery business with your family's authority from Fantasy?"

"Technically, but I'm not currently serving as an ambassador, and it involves too much complaining and paperwork to do in a single night. I just wanted to see him sweat."

"I thought you hated people knowing your Fantasy identity?"

"I do," I said, "but sometimes it's fun to throw it at people who think they're better than everyone else."

Driving to Harlem Heights for a try, there wasn't a bouncer outside, but a group of men hanging around the entrance. They gave us a look-over, frowning at my blue-green eyes, but decided to let us pass. Maybe because my car and our clothes suggested that we had money to spend at their establishment.

Being interracial meant living by the standards of two different cultures while being accepted by neither of them. Meaning everyone mostly avoided the two new faces in the club. Whatever.

Being underage, I grabbed two mocktails from the bar, then we stepped back and forth, clapping to the music, commenting on particularly impressive dancers and musicians. Growing up in Fantasy and attending university in Procedural gave me plenty of dancing experience, but not in swing. On the other hand, Nita seemed more comfortable in Latin forms, leaving us confused but highly entertained as we stepped on each others' toes.

After an hour of pretending to swing, we worked up an appetite and grabbed dinner from the bar. I offered to pay for Nita's plate of Western chicken tenders, but she slid her cash across the bar first. I bought myself a Mystery entrée of wonder packets. Since the skies were still clear, we found a bench and table outside, where we could talk without shouting over the music.

"So," I began, "is your full name Anita?"

"Huh? Oh, probably not."

"Probably?"

"It's just what Truth decided to call me. Nita Incog, like a mixed up version of 'incognitus,' Latin for—"

"The 'unknown,'" I finished, happy to find a use for my Latin studies. "But Truth hates aliases. Are you that mysterious to her?" I buckled down like an eager conspirator.

"I'm that mysterious to everyone, including myself." Nita stared at me, deadly serious.

My smile died. "Oh. Amnesia?"

Nita nodded and busied herself with her meal. Her eyes refused to meet mine when she looked up. I hoped that it was simply entertainment from our surroundings—not discomfort—that kept her attention from me.

I'd initially asked her out with hopes of getting to know her. How was this supposed to work, then? If she'd anticipated this conversation, it made a little more sense why she'd shut me down.

"If you don't mind me asking—" I hesitated, unsure how painful the subject was "—what's the first thing you remember?"

"Waking up terrified and confused in a hospital."

I winced. "How old—oh wait, I guess you wouldn't know. How long ago then?"

She met my eyes for the briefest of glances. "Six months ago. All I know is what was on my check-in sheet. A lifeguard found me washed up on the shore of Lake Mishi. I had nearly drowned with severe hypothermia, but was otherwise un-wounded. I was in the hospital for a week, and they gave me a cleaning job to pay off my bills. One month later, Truth stopped by for an investigation, and she took an interest in me. I have no memory, but I have a life-time's worth of muscle memory for fighting. Based on my combat training, Truth thinks I worked for the state. If that's the case, well, all I have to do is work my way around until someone recognizes me."

"Ah." I leaned back in my seat. "That's why you two freaked out when I kept looking at you. You thought I recognized you. Sorry, I didn't mean to mislead you."

She shrugged without a word and continued to stare at her food, as if deciding her next bite was her only interest.

"In that case," I tried again, "what do you know about yourself? I mean, you're somewhere in your early to mid-twenties? You speak fluidly with a Mysterious accent, but who's to say that you're native?"

"Your investigation skills are astounding," she murmured around her mouthful of fries.

"Hah! A joke! Then you do have a soul!"

She twitched an eyebrow and set her fork down. "You want a riddle? How's this; everyone who works for the state is cataloged, so Truth ran my fingerprints. Mine came up blank. What's that supposed to mean?"

I raised my eyebrows. "Good question. I can't tell you anything document-wise, but I can do a personal analysis. If you want anything more than 'you're somewhere in your early twenties,' you'll need to pay me for it."

"Pay you? With what?" She seemed skeptical for understandable reasons. Beautiful women like her had to be cautious.

"Another drink." I gestured to the club to mean the bar inside.

She released a small breath for my simple payment, but her skepticism remained. "What do you want?"

"Anything non-alcoholic. You choose."

She blinked, but took the bait. She stood and I escorted her back inside. She stood at the bar for six minutes before we returned to our table outside.

"Well?" she asked, setting down our two lemonades.

"Thank you," I said, "for the drink and for permission to stare at you like a stalker for my analysis."

She rocked back as I laughed with pure humor.

Gathering my breath again, I leaned closer. "Come on, you have to admit, investigators are just professional stalkers. It's basically our job description."

Her response was simply to lift an eyebrow and wait for my report.

"Alright, you paid. My turn to deliver. From my brief observation, you have an incredibly variable walk. You began sluggish, dreading, almost like a rebellious teenager. Then you straightened out with long, confident strides, like you owned the place. Your next phase was similar, but included a bit more swinging of the arms and hips. A flirty walk. You reached the bar and shifted at least three more times as you made your choice. First, you were leisurely, hip popped and shoulders tilted, then straightened up as if your boss was watching, then went into almost attention like your boss was a general. Your return was extremely balanced and light on your feet. You made no sound as your feet placed precisely on the edge of an invisible line to your destination. Forget the drinks in your hands, I could have put a full cup of water on your head without spilling a drop.

"Unfortunately, not much can be said about your choice of flavors, since lemonade is common everywhere. All in all, I'm impressed and gratified to be in your presence."

I leaned back, quite pleased with myself. Nita, however, seemed disappointed.

"Well, you've confirmed that I don't know who I am even when I walk. That's nothing new."

"I've deduced," I said, "that you had rigorous training to be anyone you want. Training that goes as deeply as the way you set your feet while you walk. Training so deep that you can't forget it even with amnesia. There's only one department that goes that deep, Nita, and they aren't trained in Mystery."

CHAPTER 12

In the unraveling of a crime, one may consistently antici-
pate a twist that adds intricacy to the pursuit of justice.
(There's always a twist.)

- *Lemuel Gulliver's Travel Guide,*
Vol. 4: Mystery
(with notes by Aeron)

Special Operations," Nita gasped. "You think I was trained
in Thriller?"

"Undercover, specifically," I added. "I bet if I asked you
to imitate an elderly woman with arthritis and an Inferno, Horror, accent, you'd have no problem."

Nita's eyes constricted in concentration. Then she hunched
over and her hands shook weakly. "Like this?" she asked in a
loud whisper, with a tone of skepticism and suspicion. "My
arthritis is in my knees, so I'll need help standing."

I shivered and laughed nervously. "That accent is far too
close for comfort. Please don't ever speak that way again."

Her posture returned as she released a true smile. I just
about melted at the sight of it.

As much as I wanted to bask in the moment, I played it
cool and waved it off. "There you go. Of course, that was only

with a small sample of you walking back and forth from the bar. With your permission to analyze you a little longer…"

"No," she said, but she still smiled.

I counted her continued smile as another point of victory. We sat in silence for a bit, enjoying our meals.

"Well, the Horror accent…" she said between bites, "I recognize it faintly in some of your words. Truth said your dad is from Fantasy and your mom is from Horror?"

"I guess that much is obvious from my accents and magical ability." I stabbed one of my pastry pockets and shoved it into my mouth. "What else did she tell you?"

Nita offered a half shrug. "She told me the basics of your parentage, but why do you hide it? Aren't they influential rulers and powerful heroes? Records say you're a direct inheritor of the Margen Duchy, and that makes you, what? A noble?"

"You looked me up?" I smirked. That meant she'd been thinking about me. To answer her question, I said, "It's worse. I'm royalty. My parents are the future Duke and Duchess of Margen in Fairy, Fantasy. My great-grandfather was King of all Fairy. Now, it's my father's cousin. But it doesn't matter. I abdicated."

"Then are the records outdated?"

"Unfortunately not. My grandfather, the current Duke of Margen, won't let me officially abdicate until I turn twenty-five or he dies—whichever comes later. My sister will inherit. She doesn't believe she should rule, but she has a good heart."

"You do too," Nita whispered.

I shrugged and kept chewing to hide the pleasure that came with her compliment.

"Well, what else about you?" she urged. "You psychoanalyzed me to tell me more than I know about myself. Do I have to do the same and ask you to stand up and grab some extra napkins?"

"Sorry." I swallowed. "I'm…I'm not used to talking about myself. I guess I'm accustomed to the spirits knowing who I am. They follow me everywhere and gossip about me like I'm their monarch. It wouldn't surprise me if two or three of them are standing by and making critiques."

Nita stopped chewing.

I shrugged and looked around as if I could see them. I knew them well enough to make some educated guesses. "You have nothing to worry about. They won't do anything to you. They only tease me because I have a life. Yeah, I'm talking to you, Sherlock."

She chuckled uneasily, glancing about as if to find them. "You know Sherlock? As in Holmes?"

"Yeah, him, Hercule Poirot, Auguste Dupin, and Inspector Lestrade are some of my best Mystery friends. They like to live vicariously through me. Yeah, that one's for you, Hercule. Though he's probably hovering around the beach tonight. He tends to do that when the clouds open the way for the stars. Little Miss Drew's probably the one taking notes to critique me tonight. She's a Romantic at heart."

Nita blinked at me with wide eyes. "Well, then. When you name drop, you really name drop. With resources like those, you'll probably be pulled onto the Sponsor Case like Truth and I were."

"You think so?" I asked, hoping not to sound too eager. "Although, considering the incident in the tunnel with Sponsor's number one, I wonder if I'm really cut out for this."

Nita shook her head slightly. "It shouldn't have happened. They knew exactly what route we'd take and ambushed us. I suspect information was leaked."

"You think there's a mole?" I asked. "Who?"

Another little shake. "There are too many options. Anyone on the police force could have shared the information—willingly or not. You can bet it wasn't me. I only ever talk to Truth, but she…well, you know how she hates secrets."

"You think that Truth is a security flaw?"

"I don't know," she said. "I want to trust Truth. She took me in and has been nothing but kind to me. Technically, the breach could be from within the chain of SSS as we report to Baldi through the secretary."

With a mocking "gotcha" snap, I teased, "The secretary. When it isn't the spouse, it's always the secretary."

Nita released a half chuckle but shook her head. "We need more information. Even if we catch Sponsor, it'll be a completely different matter proving that he's the one managing the gang businesses."

I tapped my fingers on the table in thought. "I understand that problem all too well. Since you worked on the Quigley Case, maybe you can help me with my dilemma."

Nita half shrugged. "Truth does most of the detective work, but I can try."

I answered her half shrug with a half smile. "I know who killed Richard Quigley, but I can't prove it because his murderer's dead. He was pushed off the catwalk by a poltergeist."

Nita raised her eyebrows and said nothing for a moment, thinking over my words as she drank her lemonade.

Setting down her drink, she said, "That actually makes sense. Truth had a theory to prove Mr. Quigley's innocence by showing that no one could flee down that catwalk unnoticed. With some quick trial runs, I managed it, but William Quigley doesn't have my skills. Either way, the Quigley Case is a Criminal Defense Case. You haven't been asked to solve the murder, simply prove Mr. Quigley's innocence."

I nodded reluctantly. "Yes, but as a speaker for the spirits, I feel obligated to take care of the poltergeist. He has haunted the theater for years and murdered a young boy. He needs to see justice."

Nita raised a thoughtful smirk. "Truth's right. You are who you are. You were born to rule and serve. What I don't understand is why you came to work in Mystery instead of your homeland?"

I tilted my head at her insight. I took a moment to pull on my own drink and consider how to answer. "I wanted to choose my own fate. Being an investigator in Mystery has its own responsibilities, but I chose them. As an earl, my responsibilities would keep me locked in Fairy, Fantasy, with my only ventures out being trips as an ambassador. Everything would be scheduled and reported. No more casual outings with beautiful and mysterious women." I gestured to Nita and earned a little blush. "I'd be arranged to marry my almost-cousin and every thought must serve the people. I'm just not ready to give up my life yet."

Nita blinked. "I hadn't realized royalty life could be so limiting. I remember..." She shook her head.

"You remember?" I urged her.

Her brows constricted, and she tensed her jaw as if battling with her mind.

"Well, I forget most of my dreams, and those I remember are usually about my current missions—the dangers and insane possibilities. But every once in a while, I dream of peace. Of a child running beside the feet of mountains, laughing as she runs through a forest. Though nothing's said about her, I have this gut instinct that she's a princess. Maybe she was one of my friends, or maybe it's just a weird dream. Well, either way, she seems so carefree. I figured that was how royalty lived."

I smirked. "Then you should do your homework before you try to go undercover as a royal. Their lives are anything but carefree. Isn't it funny how we think the problems of others are easier than our own?"

"What do you mean?"

"You don't have anyone to care for but yourself. And you don't even know who you are. I doubt this is how you see it, but that sounds like freedom to me."

"Freedom?" Nita's eyes widened.

"The ultimate. You can go anywhere, do anything, be anyone. Have you ever considered becoming an actress? With your skills, you'd be incredible!"

She grinned with a far-off look. "Well, the thought crossed my mind."

I reached over with excitement. "You should try it! You could do your own stunts and everything!"

She laughed, a musical sound. It wasn't like the twinkling bells of fairies with their tricks, or giggly like the girls who swooned over my every word. Nita's laugh was full of heart.

She looked down and faltered. In my excitement, I'd reached over and taken her hand. My insides squirmed as I forced myself to keep it there.

While I had the nerve, I convinced myself to go for it.

"Nita, you could be anyone in the world, yet you chose to aid a private investigator. You chose to use your skills to help others. I think that's incredible, that you're incredible."

She met my eyes and didn't say anything. She didn't need to. For the first time, she seemed to see herself from my eyes. Her eyes reflected my amazement and how beautiful she was to me.

She blinked rapidly and pulled her hand away from mine. "What time is it? I should probably get home?"

Yes, more people left the club than entered it in the last hour, and the music tones seemed to say, "Good night." But that didn't explain Nita's sudden urge to go home.

"Nita—"

"Well, I indulged you," she said, gathering her purse and standing with her back to me, "but I stand by my earlier statement; I don't hang out with people."

"But—"

"Well, up till now I haven't acquainted myself with anyone who genuinely wanted to befriend me—other than Truth, so maybe my statement needs to be amended."

I stood to join her side. When she turned around, her eyes jolted wide to find me standing so close. Her breath stuttered, and I smiled at the rare moment of catching her off guard.

She stared at me, her breath suspended, too tense for the simple task of gathering her possessions. Supernaturals, she was beautiful. Without breaking eye contact, I reached around her to lift her jacket from the chair. I had to bend a little to reach it, bringing our lips threateningly close. With her jacket in hand, I straightened and offered it to her. Her eyes flashed with various expressions at her jacket: surprise, relief, disappointment...

She took her jacket and a conscious step away, avoiding my eyes. "Well, I need to keep my relationships professional until I know who I am, investigators or not. You say I'm a special operative from Thriller, but for all I know, I'm just a lost woman who helped her grandma solve mysteries from her kitchen in Cozy. Now, she has no one but her cat to help her solve the Cases."

I sighed. Then that was her deal. "We can't let the cat do all the work."

She straightened again, transformed back into the all-business Investigations Combat Specialist Nita.

"Thank you for dinner. I would appreciate it if you could drop me off at my apartment now."

I nodded and led the way, keeping my hands in my pockets. The silence of the walk to my car continued during the drive, with the small exceptions of asking for directions.

"Right here," she said, pointing at a tall apartment complex. I pulled over and settled my car in one of the limited guest parking spots.

"Um, Spade?"

"Yes?" I looked over as I unbuckled my seatbelt. She stared with wide eyes and was positioned ready to bolt out the door.

"Well, I had a nice time and all, but I'm not going to invite you up."

"What—whoa, no, that's—" I couldn't help it, I laughed. It was a relief to tease again. "No, I'm just parking to open your door and ensure you make it inside. I know it's not common in Contemporary lands, but I like to treat women with the less-common courtesies."

Her cheeks reddened, embarrassed that she'd been the forward-minded one. I stepped out and rounded my car to open her door. She still blushed, but accepted my hand to help her stand from the seat.

I grinned. "I mean, I still want a hug goodnight." She eyed me warily, and I clarified, "Between friends."

She rolled her eyes and indulged me with a goodnight hug. She probably meant it to be loose and quick, but I lingered. She didn't wear perfume, but Supernaturals, she smelled nice. I let go and stepped back before the temptation to linger longer became too strong.

"In all seriousness," I said, "you should try out for a play. I think you'd be a star."

She smiled, ending our evening on a high note. "Goodnight, Spade."

CHAPTER 13

Why, pray tell, do acts of murder oft manifest in multiples?
The resolution of one crime oftentimes proves instrumental
in elucidating another. (More crimes are often committed to
cover the first. Here's a thought; don't commit the first!)

- *Lemuel Gulliver's Travel Guide,*
Vol. 4: Mystery
(with notes by Aeron)

As soon as my spirit rose from my sleeping body that night, guilt piggy-backed onto my pleasure regarding my outing with Nita.

Margaret.

Curses, it was hard to keep relationships straight with only half of my memories during the day. But why did I feel guilty? Nita had been the one to instigate the outing, and she'd made it very clear that she wasn't interested in romance.

I remembered vague impressions as I drove to Margaret's abandoned house and set up my bedding in her dusty front room. Memories of conversations and movements became clearer as I stood in her humble home. I remembered only a portion of her beauty, but was jarringly reminded as soon as she greeted me in my sleep.

She curtsied. "Good night, Mr. Spade."

"I thought I asked you to call me Aeron?" I asked.

"Aeron." She pinched back a shy smile. "How may I be of help to you? Are you comfortable?"

"I'm comfortable enough to sleep at least this long. Thanks for letting me stay here. If you could just watch over my body, I need to confront your nasty neighbor in the theater."

"Of course, Aeron," she said with another curtsy. "Please, be careful. I'll be waiting for you."

I was about to slip out when another thought struck me. "Actually, there might be something else you could do to help. The police caught a man who is supposedly one of Sponsor's higher ups. His name is James Clay. Would you be able to track him down?"

Her eyes widened with excitement. "Of course! Gladly! I shall be back before you can even miss me."

"Doubtful," I murmured. I wasn't sure if she heard me, but she bit her lip as if she had.

I graced her with a warm smile before we each slipped through opposite walls. Outside, the stars shone brightly. I hoped that they'd continue to shine through the night in case I needed to repeat last night's struggle to cross the threshold without my ghostly vision. I'd set my alarm to repeat the exorcism that night if my conversations as a spirit failed. I prayed to the Supernaturals that my words would reach Neil and I wouldn't be forced to exorcize the poltergeist without answers.

I drifted into the backroom workshop, eyes open and wary. The poltergeist sat at the props table behind the stage set, scratching a deep gash into the wood. He looked every bit the part of a mad spirit, dressed in ragged clothes from another century, consumed with his work. He didn't even see me when I entered.

Even if I included his dead years, how was he only thirty-five years old? I could excuse the clothes as a costume, but his skin sagged with wrinkles, and his eyes were sunken black holes. While most spirits chose to appear younger than their death age, he chose to look older. Why?

I cleared my throat. "Neil Martin."

He jerked up and stood. The chair actually moved back as he did.

"You came back," he said. His eyes flickered through several emotions before he cautiously asked, "Who are you? You're a spirit, but your body was alive in the green room two nights ago."

"As I said before, I'm Aeron Spade, the Haunted." Our conversation twisted my mind in more than one way. I rarely met spirits who didn't know about me. Obviously, Neil was linked to the theater and didn't get out much. The other oddity was the mere existence of a get-to-know-you conversation with a poltergeist. Yes, I felt like I walked on the eggshells of a hostage negotiation, but at least we were talking. "I'm from Fantasy," I continued. "I have an ability to visit the dead in my sleep, then return to the living to serve both realms. I'm investigating the death of Richard Quigley—"

Neil didn't let me say another word as his fury exploded at me. So much for our cooperative conversation. He flipped the entire table over, then picked up the props to throw them at me.

No matter that I was only a spirit. The sight of teacups and saucers flying at my face made me flinch. What a temperament. I hadn't even finished my introduction and he was angry at me? What had I done to earn such hatred?

"Get out! Leave me alone!" he screamed.

"What's wrong with you?" I returned, trying my best to restrain my own frustration. "Why do you drive everyone away? Why did you kill Richard?"

Another saucer soared at me.

"Why are you here?" I demanded. "Why do you haunt the occupants of this theater instead of returning to Paranormal?"

Neil screamed a wretched sound of the condemned, grabbing the entire chair and smashing it to the table. "I WAS MURDERED HERE!"

Curses, if he was that powerful in Mystery, I feared his capabilities in Paranormal. I backed through the walls to leave the stage and theater. Neil continued to rage inside.

A piece of it finally made sense. Malignant spirits were usually malignant people in life, but in some cases they became malignant when crying for justice. Neil Martin had been murdered in the theater, but the theater had no other listings for foul play. He'd never received justice for his death. That linked him to the scene and fueled his anger.

I wouldn't get anything from him concerning the Quigley Case until his own Case was solved. Curses, I didn't have time to research a death that probably had no reports. But it might be my only option. Neil's words after killing Richard had been, "better than nothing." If I could find Neil's true goal, then maybe I could find his motive for killing Richard.

Visiting the populated rehearsal room, I asked if anyone had witnessed Neil's murder.

"Nay," said the Renaissance director. "His life did end ere my demise."

I frowned. "He died seventeen years ago."

He raised his eyebrows with all the interest of a nobleman hearing of the poorhouses. "Verily? A decade past, my mortal life did cease."

My eyes narrowed. "Then why do you talk like you're ancient?"

"I revel in the dulcet cadence of the Renaissance's discourse."

Sighing, I rubbed my forehead. Actors.

"Fine," I said, "but at least someone must have witnessed his death."

"Nay," he repeated. "As a specter, Mr. Neil did afright the former spirits of this playhouse, and thus banished them with his temperament."

Great, then I'd need to hunt down the previous residents… supposing they hadn't moved on to the Unknown Beyond.

I flew back to Margaret's house at the same hidden angle I had come in case Neil decided to follow me.

Floating through the doorway, I paused at the sight that greeted me. Margaret hadn't noticed me yet. Her eyes were fixed on my body, a hint of worry in her silver eyes. She rested her translucent hand on top of my physical hand. I didn't feel it. I floated nearer, and she snapped her hand away.

"Mr. Spade! What happened? Your body trembled, like you were scared or in pain. Only in these last few minutes have you calmed again."

"Please, just Aeron," I said. "I'm calm now because I saw you watching over me."

"Aeron." She bit her lip. "Forgive me."

"There's no need to be embarrassed. Thank you," I said, wanting to rest a hand on her arm. "Did you find any information on James Clay?"

Her mouth twisted with disappointment. "I was able to locate multiple men by the name of James Clay, though none of them struck me as followers of Sponsor. One was a dad patiently taking his turn to put his baby to sleep, and another seemed to be a journalist, working through these midnight hours for a newspaper column. If any, I might suspect the one man who snored an awful ruckus—enough to make his wife sleep with a pillow over her ears."

I suppressed a smile at her analysis. "It's possible the man we caught used a fake ID, but thank you for looking into them.

Then for watching over me. No one's looked after me so intently before."

"No one?" She shyly raised her eyes to mine. "With your many suitresses?"

I grimaced. "I don't know if 'many' is the right numerical adjective—"

"According to the spirits, your first kiss was Princess Ceinwen Thunderhelm of Erebor, Middle Novel, yet you seemed to make efforts to avoid her after."

"E-ehh," I stuttered. Apparently, when she said she knew about my past courtships, she meant that she knew *all* about my past courtships. "I avoided her because we were thirteen and awkward then, and now we're awkward because I tower over her." She was half-dwarf, after all.

"You seemed to focus on a new woman every year, however, some stuck around a bit longer," she continued. "You boondoggled with the elven Lady Mylaela of Rivendale, but I have a theory that t'was more of an attempt to please your parents. Only the dead know about the time you nearly courted Princess Sophia from Children's. You briefly returned to Princess Thunderhelm, but that was short-lived. Hah. Did you catch that pun?" She paused to grin at me as I gaped. While Neil knew nothing about me, this woman was on the opposite spectrum. She knew *everything*.

"While at university in Mystery, you had three more almost-serious courtships though I mix up their names. Then 'twas announced that you briefly courted Princess Cateline Sayer last year, which I believe was more for politics since she is your second cous—"

"Alright, I've courted several women," I cut her off. Curses, that was humiliating. Did this woman have the tabloids memorized? I'd never felt guilty about dating a lot until an attractive woman counted them off. At least she only mentioned the women I'd kissed, and I only kissed those I courted exclusively.

My serious relationships never lasted longer than a season or two, giving me plenty of time to explore options, feigning the "single and loving it" life while feeling lonely and frustrated. Hence last year's political relationship with my father's cousin's daughter to bolster Fairy Kingdom's patriotism.

If Margaret followed my dating life so closely, how long until she heard about my recent outing with Nita? Would she misinterpret it as a date? What would Margaret think if I showed interest in herself?

I sighed and sat in the air. "I like women, and they seem to like me, but I never manage to go beyond that in a relationship. I'm caught between what I want and what I need."

Margaret tilted her head with curiosity, then slipped her legs under to sit in the air across from me. "I know 'tis not my place to ask, but if you want to talk, I will listen."

I gave her a sad half-smile. "That's more than I can say for any of my living friends. See, I enjoy my time here as a spirit, but I need to be alive to make my time as a spirit useful. I want to be free to fall in love with whomever, choose my own career, and make my own life, but I need to marry another royal—or at least a noble—for the future when my life is chosen for me as a duke."

She said nothing while I set out my thoughts and weighed them against each other. Deep in thought, she took an extra minute to ponder before speaking. "What do you need for yourself, not for those whom you're responsible?"

I sat back and thought on that, pulling ideas from my earlier conversation with Nita. "I need to be free. Not free from responsibilities, but free to choose my responsibilities. That's why I want to be an investigator of Mystery so badly. I was born into the responsibilities of an earl. My ability forced me into a responsibility to care for the spirits. I don't mind serving the people and spirits, but can't I choose *how* I serve them? I want to serve the living and dead by solving their Cases. I want *that* responsibility."

She nodded. "And of your responsibility to select a future duchess? Can you not fill your want and need by falling in love with a royal or noble?"

I gave her a dubious smirk. "You know my courting history. Most of them were royal or noble. I tried falling in love with princesses. For one reason or another, it falls apart, but it's usually because nobles don't understand my desires to labor among the common folk. Also, they can't ever 'just be friends.' Every noble or royal relationship—Romantic or not—comes with a package of politics and alliances to tiptoe around."

"Then your shift to dating commoners when you came to Mystery wasn't because of your limited options for nobles, but because of your lack of interest," she concluded. "You prefer common girls over noblewomen."

I blinked at her directness. I kind of liked it. I didn't need to guess what was on her mind. And her conclusion wasn't wrong.

"I don't dislike noblewomen," I said, "just their social norms. I want to fall in love naturally. I want to be her friend and slowly build trust and loyalty until we're both puppy-dog sweet for each other. I want to let it deepen and mature until the craziness burns with a passion that we decide to spend the rest of our lives together. Then, for it to never fade away as we share secrets with only a wink while we eat dinner or read books on the same sofa." Like I'd seen my parents do.

Margaret bit her lip and turned her eyes down to her hands in her lap. "Why, Mr. Spade, you are a Romantic."

I smirked. "Half Fantastic and half Horror actually, but my parents met in Romance, so maybe some of that leaked in."

"Yes, I know your heritage," she said.

"With everything else you know about me, I'm not surprised. But now, you know more about me than most people from this conversation." My words flowed without thought as I said, "I've appreciated this time to become acquainted. Did you reach the puppy-dog stage before I did?"

She gasped a little as her eyes snapped up to mine. Beautiful silver. Staring at them long enough would probably send me beyond the puppy-dog level, but a distant thought warned me to hold off. It would only make me feel more guilty when I'd think of Nita during the day… Nita, who refused to flirt back; Nita, who refused to consider a future until she discovered her past.

As beautiful and intriguing as Nita was, I redirected my attentions to the beautiful and open woman in front of me. She was definitely worth my attentions.

She bit her bottom lip, drawing my eyes to their fullness.

"Maybe," I said, "after I'm done with this Case, you can join me for my other Cases. I've appreciated your help on this and with Sponsor's man."

She gasped again, this time with excitement and without shyness. "Yes, please. I would like that very much."

Her innocent grin was beautiful enough to kiss.

Before I could do anything too brazen, loud beeping jostled my consciousness.

My alarm woke me two hours before sunrise again. I lay still on Ms. Norris' couch for a moment longer to remember my dream. Margaret. I smiled, grateful to remember her name and appearance even after I woke. I had a brief flash of Neil's angry charge at me, but the main picture that stayed with me was Ms. Norris' smile. Margaret. If I had the choice, I would have laid there thinking of her or—better yet—gone back to sleep. Unfortunately, I had work to do.

144

I sat up and wrote down the most important thoughts from my sleep that I couldn't let myself forget. Guarding myself with my emergency pack, aspergillum of holy water, and a box of matches, I walked to the theater again.

I grumbled to myself, wondering what I would possibly do differently tonight. If not, then I was the definition of insanity bordering stupidity: performing the same action over and over while hoping for different results.

Reaching the back door, I went through the same process of convincing myself to walk through the dark to turn on the lights in the workshop again. Curses, I needed to resolve this Case tonight simply to save myself from repeating the trauma.

Just as I bolstered enough courage to lift my foot forward, a flashlight beamed through the darkness, and the lights flipped on.

"Oh, it's you." The security guard visibly relaxed. "Look, I don't know if tonight's a good night for you to be snooping around. The Regal Ghost already made a mess of the stage. I swear, I'm not making it up. He—"

"Tipped over a backdrop, broke several tea sets, and bashed the chair against the table. I know."

The man's face went a tint lighter. "The other guard said you was somethin' else, but—dang, you're good. If you just got here, how'd you know all that?"

"If you don't know," I said, "then it'll be too complicated for me to explain right now. Can you give me a moment alone with the crime scene?" I really wanted the stage and pits, but asking for the crime scene made more sense for what the security expected me to do.

"Sure, sure," he said, nodding and pointing the way before retreating to the monitor room.

Defending myself with my holy water, I walked through the workshop, alone as far as the living could tell.

"Neil Martin?" I called, daring him to meet me. "You told me that you were murdered here. I understand that you're upset without justice for your murder, but killing that boy wasn't the answer… Neil Martin!"

Reaching the threshold between the workshop and stage, everything went black. Neil had turned off the lights. I was in the middle of the room with no walls or sense of direction in the darkness. No, as my heartbeat quickened and eyes adjusted, I could see the stage ahead with its ghost light. Even as I stared at the faint blue light, a scream howled through the auditorium and shattered the bulb.

The blackness that surrounded me was worse than the tunnel. There were no windows, no lights at the end. It was worse than stepping across the back door threshold into the darkness. I was in the darkness with no light behind me to show me the way out. No shadows or shaded silhouettes told me which direction to go for the light switches. No walls or barriers for support. For all I knew, there were no light switches. I no longer stood in the workshop of the Regal Theater. I stood in the darkest pits of Horror.

The Shadow of the Valley of Death had come to kill me again.

My skin shivered, and my bones chilled with the memory of it devouring my life. I was going to die again, and no one could save me.

Screams of outright terror echoed through the room and my skull. Were they mine?

A distant whisper reminded me of my therapy sessions. It didn't matter. The fear and memory of the Valley Shadow overwhelmed all other memories.

Light broke behind my squeezed-shut eyelids. I opened them to a workshop as bright as day. Every unbroken light was turned on. There was no guard in sight.

Thank the Supernaturals no one else saw me in my pathetic state. I found myself sitting in a fetal position on the floor with my hands wrapped around my head.

Movement caught my attention from the props table. The security had "cleaned up" Neil's earlier mess of broken teacups and saucers by placing all pieces on the props table. A pencil floated above them.

Curses, Neil was still there! He could stab me with that pencil, and who knew if I'd die from the puncture or lead poisoning first?

Not waiting for the answer, I scrambled to my feet and ran out the door. There was no justifying my flight this time. I was a coward. Maybe I wasn't meant to be an investigator after all.

CHAPTER 14

In the course of investigation, there unfailingly occurs a
moment of revelation—a sudden and brilliant epiphany.
(Epiphany! A great word for a great moment.)

> - *Lemuel Gulliver's Travel Guide,*
> *Vol. 4: Mystery*
> (with notes by Aeron)

Too embarrassed to visit Margaret, I drove directly home. I stuck to the main roads with their streetlamps. Another reason I wanted to work in the big cities of Mystery was that they never went to sleep. The city lights never turned off, and the light pollution meant I'd never be completely in the dark. The sun would rise over the city skyline in an hour, meaning there wasn't enough time to visit my spiritual friends at home. There was time, however, to call my uncle.

Of my four uncles, only Lord Dunstan Fromm, the Night Shade, of Divinity, survived long enough to witness my birth. While my mom taught me with long-range weapons, and Master Bahr had taught me proper swordsmanship and hand-to-hand combat, Dunstan had taught me how to street-fight and fight dirty. He also had an ability to absorb light.

Considering the events from yesterday—before and after falling asleep—I needed another session with him.

I quickly showered and prepared for the day. As the sun's morning rays reached into my living room, I sat on my sofa and called Uncle Dunstan.

Similar to my parents' home, the city within Divinity's mountain didn't have technology for phones. My phone was connected to a communicating orb in Dunstan's drawing room. It was unlikely for him to be near, so I ate breakfast and practiced breathing techniques as I waited for him to answer.

"Hello?"

"Uncle Dunstan," I said. "How are you?"

"Aeron," he said. I could hear his smile, speaking as if everything was a tease. "How's my favorite nephew?"

I scoffed. He said that to all of his nephews.

"Tired," I said honestly. "I need another fear session."

"Another one?" he asked. "But it's only been two weeks. Ask me again and I'll think you get some kind of sick kick out of torturing yourself."

"Please," I said, snapping my bracelet on and off. "I need to learn to beat this or I'll never be able to do my job."

"Or join me on my night Adventures." He laughed. If only there wasn't truth to that joke. With an affinity for the dark, my uncle was nocturnal. That was how I knew he'd be awake before the crack of dawn.

Uncle Dunstan sighed. "Fine, I'll do it. Are you home?"

"Yes. Make it gradual."

"As you say, weirdo."

I wanted to tease him back, but I couldn't manage any levity as my heart pounded with anxiety.

Calm down, breathe.

My house lights began to dim.

Breathe…Stay calm…Calm.

I flicked on my flashlight, but its power was weak against my uncle's ability to absorb light.

"Hey," my uncle said, "this distance is hard enough without you adding to my workload."

"Sorry," I said, clicking off the flashlight.

He grunted, and my house darkened more.

Calm—stay calm.

Shadows swallowed my house and took hold of my heart.

Calm! Stay calm! B-breathe!

A memory flashed. Laying on stone as a massive shadow ate my life away.

Stop! It was just a memory! It wasn't real! It wasn't happening again! I wasn't going to die again!

Somewhere between the quick breaths and tremors, I heard my uncle's voice.

"Aeron? Stay with me, Aeron. Do you want me to stop?"

Yes. With his disembodied voice in the darkness, he could have been sitting next to me. I imagined he was. I pretended I wasn't alone.

"No," I said. "I—I…"

"What are you afraid of, Aeron?" he asked calmly, knowing the answer. "The darkness reminds you of the time you nearly died, right?"

Yes, but there'd been no "nearly" about it. I had died. The shadow had sucked away my life.

"But you're not afraid of death, right, Aeron?" my uncle asked, soft as the night. "You've told me before. You see death every night in your sleep."

I swallowed back the saliva nearly drowning me, trying to remember what he would ask next. We went through a similar script every time, letting the routine become a mantra of calm.

I hadn't answered, so he rephrased his line, "What are you truly afraid of, Aeron?"

150

The unknown. After a few shaking breaths, I managed to say it aloud.

"Yeah, which is bullbegging normal," he said with a light chuckle. "People fear me because I can create darkness. But am I a scary person?"

Considering the time he tried to kill my father and his mastery of multiple martial art styles, yes, he was once known as the Night Terror. But he shed that title before I was born and never looked back. He even went as far as becoming a priest until the people called him the Night Shade again.

"No," I said.

"You hesitated, but thanks," he chuckled. "The darkness scares people because they rely too much on their sight. But you can still listen. Listen to your breathing. Listen to my voice. Listen and feel. Feel your clothing. Feel your chair. Tell me what you feel."

I could definitely hear my gasping breaths, but I could also feel the tweed sofa. I described its scratchy but durable fabric to my uncle.

"Good. Now, your mother has a lot of sayings about how to survive Horror, but there's a specific one about fears that's not in her brother's book. Do you know what I'm talking about?"

"I—I don't remember."

"Yes, you do," he softly urged. "It's there, but you're letting your fear block the memory. What does she say about being prepared?"

Yes, I remembered. I swallowed again and tried to take a steadying breath. "There's nothing to fear i-if you're prepared."

"Right. If you prepare for a situation, no matter how terrifying it might be, you can handle it. You can rarely control your situation, but you can always control yourself. How's your breathing?"

"Faster than normal," I said, "but I'm not hyperventilating."

"We'll call that improvement," he said, and my lights dawned back on as if nothing had happened. My whole body shook from tension. I willed myself to relax, muscle by muscle.

"Aeron?" Uncle Dunstan asked from the phone. "You're alright?"

"Yeah," I said, grabbing a coloring book from the nightstand beside my couch. It felt juvenile, but coloring helped me to relax. I stabbed a bright green pencil at the paper and scribbled at a section of the foreground.

"You still sound stressed," he said. "It's okay to be scared, but you can't let the fear control you."

"I know!" I said, jabbing my pencil hard enough to rip the paper and chip the pencil. "It's been fifteen years! I'm a grown man just trying to get a job! I shouldn't have to deal with this anymore. I know there's nothing waiting in the darkness. I know I'm not in Horror. I know the Valley Shadow isn't here to eat me again, but…but I can't."

My usually jovial uncle didn't say anything as I replaced the broken green pencil with a sharpened yellow. I began a different section of the background.

"Hey," he said, "there's a saying your father likes to quote, 'whether you say you can or can't, you'll be right.' Don't ask for another fear session until I'm with you in person. You do better when you have someone with you."

I scoffed. "Who would be here with me? I live alone, and there's no way I'm asking anyone to come over and hold my hand in the dark. I can't always rely on someone else, so I need to get over this by myself."

"As you say," my uncle said, and I imagined him smirking with a dramatic eye-roll. "But seriously, don't ask me again unless you have someone with you. Everyone needs support, and your parents aren't the only ones worried about you up there. Mystery's a weird place."

"Didn't you call me a weirdo earlier?" I said, finally calming down enough to test a smile. "I think that means I should fit in."

He laughed. "I guess so. Was there anything else you wanted me to do to torture you? I could whisper unintelligible words or tell you dad-jokes."

"Please, no," I laughed back. "Anything but that."

With the sun rising and his bedtime nearing, we ended the call with best wishes. I remained on my couch for a few more minutes, considering other ways to keep yesterday's incidents from repeating. Neil had caught me off guard last night. If I was to do the same to him, I needed to know more about him. Hopefully his files from Paranormal had arrived. Only one way to find out.

The thought of running into Nita again lightened my heart before I smacked it down. Margaret. I was courting Margaret. Kind of. Right? I didn't remember kissing her—and I would remember kissing her, because I really wanted to. Even if Nita fascinated me, she didn't have an interest in special interests. Unlike Margaret.

I drove to Shigaqua's Personal Records Center, smiling with thoughts of a beautiful spirit, then forcing myself to focus on the terrifying spirit when I arrived.

As my bad luck would have it, the mail hadn't arrived yet. Nancy told me to come back in an hour, shooing me to make way for others. Wandering across the street to the police department, I considered how to kill the time. I cursed my luck (fortunate and unfortunate) that Truth and Nita were there again. Truth was busy comparing notes with a detective, and I spotted Nita by the water cooler, refilling two water bottles. Would she treat me differently after our outing? I hoped not. I wanted to learn more about her—as a friend, of course. We could still be friends, right?

I could allow myself ten minutes with Nita while waiting for the mail to arrive. Then I'd really need to crack on the Case. I only had three days left, including today. But while waiting for more information…

I approached and greeted Nita with a friendly, "Hey. How's Truth doing?"

Nita turned to me with the slightest hint of raised eyebrows. "Morning, Spade. Do you always ask women about other women the day after taking them dancing?"

"I-uh, she was shot." I fumbled. I'd started with the friendly, undirected topic, expecting Nita to be cold and indifferent about our outing.

Nita's lips went thin as she bit back a teasing smile. "Don't worry, Spade. I already knew you were a flirt."

"I—what? I'm—"

"And I'm a coldhearted amnesiac, and Truth's a workaholic who won't let a little grazing keep her from catching crooks. So, now that we've stated the obvious, was there anything else you wanted to know?"

I sputtered, unsure how to move forward from the awkwardness. Why did nothing go as planned with this woman? Fine, then forget subtleties and jump. I recomposed myself and returned the tease with a sly smile. "Yes, actually. There's a lot I still want to know. About you. I want to help you discover yourself."

She barely raised her eyebrows. "What do you mean? You want to help me remember my past?"

"Not exactly. I want to help you discover who you are now."

"I know who I am now. That's not the problem."

"Is it?" I asked. "What's your favorite color?"

"Well, I don't know."

"Come on, that's not something you need to know from birth. Don't you prefer one color over the others?"

"I don't think so. Why does it matter?"

I shrugged and threw her a playful grin. "It doesn't. It's just fun. It says something about your personality. What color is your toothbrush?"

"Excuse me?"

"Your toothbrush. What color is it? You brushed your teeth this morning, right?"

"Yeah, but, well, does that mean it's my favorite color? It's…white."

"That's either very intriguing or very boring." I smiled like a Cheshire cat. "It doesn't need to be your favorite color, but it can be."

Her eyes narrowed slightly. "Alright, then what's the color of your toothbrush?"

"It used to be blue, but was bleached from sitting in direct sunlight."

She pinched her lips as she held back a smirk. "And you mocked my white?"

"Hey," I said, "I happen to like faded blue. Light blues, gray, silver, hazy white…shades of ghosts, you know?"

"You're weird," she said, though her face struggled against her suppressed smirk.

I leaned forward and grinned. "I know I am, but what are you?"

Her eyebrows twitched at my twist of the childish phrase. It seemed that she responded the most to surprises, but I expected that she was rarely surprised. How about another one?

"What do you like on your burgers?"

"My burgers?"

"Yeah."

She half shrugged. "Well, same as everyone else, I guess. Meat. Lettuce. Cheese."

"Tomatoes?" I prodded. "Pickles? Chips?"

"Chips?" she repeated.

"Yeah," I said. "I've never tried it, but I've heard good things about the texture."

Her suppressed smirk returned. "Well, sounds like you have some self-discovery to do, too."

"Sounds like a plan," I said. "I can bring the supplies if you provide the kitchen. You and Truth are boarding together, right? She's welcome to join us."

Nita raised a slow eyebrow at me. "When?"

"How about tomorrow? I'll probably need a good lunch break between my Case research."

"Tomorrow?" she asked, then shook her head. "You're relentless."

"That wasn't a 'no.'" I inflected my voice toward hope. I didn't want her to say 'no,' but I wanted her to commit.

She released a steady breath and glared at me a little. "Fine. But it isn't a hang out, it's a…it's an experiment." Though her face was impassive, her voice cringed, not believing her own lie.

"Whatever helps you sleep at night. See you tomorrow." I left her with a wave and a wink, stepping away to bother Ross next. He sat clicking away at his desk's typewriter.

"Ross," I said, "are you busy or can you help me kill another half hour?"

"Hey, Digger," he said, tearing off and filing away his typed list of names with personal information. "Sorry. Authorized eyes only."

"Ooh," I said, threatening to sneak a peek at the paper. He smacked my hand away. I laughed and pulled a chair over to sit on the other side of his desk. He had a fresh issue of *Shigaqua*

Times with a circled headline, "Arrest Attempt Goes Array in Tunnel Shooting."

"Have there been any other leads on Sponsor?"

Ross grumbled. "He's ghosting us. Hey, speaking of ghosts, could you find him?"

I scratched my chin, having a vague memory of Margaret's gift for finding people. "I have a vague recollection of asking someone to look for him. I don't remember feeling excited about her results, so it's possible he had a fake ID. I might be able to work with a depiction from a sketch artist, but you'll likely catch him first. Everything yesterday seemed to go perfectly according to plan until it suddenly didn't."

Ross scoffed. "A fake ID? Go figure. It was almost like they'd planned for us to snatch him and drive that exact route."

I frowned. "Do you think there's a mole?"

"Shoot, I hope not," he muttered. "I can't afford to think like that. The only way cops survive is by trusting each other. We're in it together for justice, not for fame and glory. Those who want money go into PI businesses. Even the suspicion of a mole can cause rifts and paranoia."

I grunted. My mom had raised me with a heavy dose of paranoia, influencing my decision to work as a lone-wolf investigator rather than a buddy-cop detective. Even if I got into the Silent Sleuth Services, I'd mostly work alone.

Spying across the street, I spotted a mail truck stopping at City Hall.

"Oh, time to hie!" I said, sliding my chair back where I found it. "I'll see what my friends can do about locating Sponsor or any of his minions. As one of them would say, 'toodle-pip!'"

Ross narrowed his eyes. "Which means…?"

"Basically, 'see you later.'"

He chuckled and reached for his work papers. "Later, Digger."

One of my law professors once said that anyone running through a police station was never a good sign, so I skipped. Passing Nita on my way out, I winked at her bewildered stare.

"Don't forget, lunch tomorrow at your place."

Nita wasn't the only one I left staring, but I didn't care. Let them wonder. When in Mystery…

Back at the records center, Nancy set a box on the counter for me. It was small enough to hold a single pair of shoes. There were no shoes inside, but papers, old photos, and a film roll.

I studied the film roll. It was labeled as, "Rehearsal," and dated seventeen years ago. That would have been the year of his death.

"Is there somewhere I can watch this?"

Nancy pointed up the stairs. "I think we keep the filmstrip projector in an empty office?"

"Thanks. I should be done with these before the day's over."

Following her directions to the spare office room, I asked a custodian to help me set up the filmstrip, projector, and sound tube.

The film began with rolling white with sporadic spots until a countdown ended with blackness. A light turned on, spot-lighting the center of an empty stage and theater house. A young man stepped into the light and looked directly at the camera, near the source of the light. He wore a black doublet with a black undershirt and tall boots that covered most of his poofy black trousers.

"Is it rolling?" Neil's living voice asked across the distance, exiting through the sound tube. He sounded completely different. Young, eager…happy.

"It's rolling," a closer voice replied. The camera man? Did I recognize that voice?

A young woman entered the scene from the side. I think they called it stage-right?

Neil turned to her and dramatically cried out, "The fair Ophelia!—Nymph, in thy horizons!"

"It's 'orisons,'" the closer voice corrected.

Neil stuck out his tongue at the camera. "Quiet on the set."

"Be nice," the young woman said, slapping his arm with a tease. Hold on, did I recognize her too?

They continued with Act 3, Scene 1 of "Hamlet," Neil playing the lead role with regular corrections from the camera man while the woman played Ophelia, receiving only encouragement. She smiled straight at the camera, squinting in the spotlight.

"From the top now," Neil said, then cleared his throat. "To be, or not to be; that is the question…"

The woman stepped out of the spotlight while Neil performed the most famous of soliloquies. I didn't know much about acting beyond undercover work, but I could see Neil's talent. Despite the camera man's corrections, Neil had a contagious emotional range to pull the viewer into the scene. He paced the stage like a man in conflict with himself, or—no—he wasn't pacing. He was following the spotlight. The light moved before Neil did.

Before I could wonder if they had a predetermined path for the scene, Neil shouted, "Hey! Are you falling asleep up there? Why are you sweeping the stage with me?"

"The scene's better with you pacing."

I frowned. Had there been a name in there? I stopped the reel and practically took the whole thing apart just to rewind it a few seconds. Putting it back together and amplifying the sound, I listened. "Willy? Hey! Are you falling asleep up there?"

Willy? As in William Quigley? Yes, that was where I recognized that voice. And the woman playing Ophelia had been Barbara Quigley. Neil knew the Quigleys?

Supernaturals. If there was a light bulb above my head, it would have cheesily lit up. This film was the key evidence.

CHAPTER 15

Not all conclusions bear a semblance of joy. At times, justice remains elusive, the "hero" fails to secure the affections of the lady fair, or the demarcation betwixt victim and culprit becomes a nebulous divide.
(...I don't like the sound of that...)

- Lemuel Gulliver's Travel Guide,
Vol. 4: Mystery
(with notes by Aeron)

Night fell, and my spirit rose from my sleeping body on Margaret's couch. Margaret floated on the other side of the room, her expressions shifting between aloofness and tenderness. Seeing me "wake," she dropped into an awkward curtsy. "Mr. Spade."

I frowned at her formality. "What happened to Aeron?"

"Fair question. What did happen to him?"

"I'm right here," I said, gesturing with my hands to be as open as possible.

"No, you're not the same Aeron whom I met last night. He was honest and true. You…" She chewed on her lip, then huffed. "You planned another date with that stone-hearted amnesiac."

"Nita?" I asked. "I wouldn't define our outing as a date; it was unplanned. She paid for herself, and she initiated it begrudgingly. Then our burgers experiment isn't a date. Truth will be there—"

"Having a chaperone does not exclude it as a courtship," she said. "I… I mind little if you have friends who are female, even pretty women, but… I thought we had connected these last two nights… maybe even bonded a little."

Her voice whispered into silence.

I swallowed hard. Curses, she looked torn. It likewise tore my heart to see her so disheartened.

"I'm sorry," I said, immediately earning her attention again. "I struggle to remember everything that I experience while I sleep, and I hadn't even met you when I first asked Nita on a date. Yes, Nita and I went out for drinks and dancing last night, then I bought dinner because I was starving, but we're not dating. She made it very clear that it wouldn't happen again. She was just helping me to relax after a traumatizing event. As for tomorrow's lunch, I want to help her as a friend, because, honestly, I'm slightly terrified to have her as an enemy."

Margaret wrung her hands together shyly. "Even with those you date…you only want friendship? Then what of last night? The words you said to me. Were those just words of a friend, thanking me for letting you sleep here?"

"No."

She raised an expressively doubtful eyebrow.

I sighed heavily. "Will you make me say it out loud?"

Her expression remained. Apparently.

"I like you, Margaret," I said. "I think you're beautiful, sweet, and that you deserved more in life."

Her mouth and eyes widened. Before she could say anything, though, I flustered on. "I could spend the night telling you how kind and thoughtful you are, but I have work to do, so…I need to talk to the poltergeist, but when I'm done, I'll come back."

I backed through the wall and left her gaping at my exit. What else could I say? I couldn't leave her thinking that I'd used her, but I only had tonight and tomorrow night to solve this Case. I was running out of time. I'd have more time to spend with Margaret after the Case was solved.

Making my way over to the Regal Theater, I replayed my uncle Dunstan's words of advice. I didn't need to be afraid if I was prepared. I was prepared by knowing who my target was; his backstory and motivations. I also didn't need to worry about the darkness as I floated into the backstage workshop with my ghostly sight to see in the dark.

"You came back?"

People and ghosts didn't need to say "boo" to startle others. I found Neil floating high on a non-existent chair with his leg and arms crossed, staring directly at the doorway where I'd come. He'd been waiting for me.

"Yes. I have a job to do."

He simply stared down at me. "You're the bravest coward I've ever seen. You were pathetic yesterday."

I cringed. "I know. You cannot be brave without first knowing fear," I said, quoting one of my favorite Fantasy sayings. Yet the lights had returned that night with no guards in sight. "Were you the one who turned on the lights again? Why?"

He turned his face away with a disdainful sniff. "As I said, you were pathetic."

Sympathy? From a poltergeist?

As much as I hated the topic, the conversation gave me hope. If we could talk, maybe I could finally get some answers. However, if I wanted him to be honest and open with me, I needed to be the same. "I'm afraid of the dark," I confessed. As much as I wanted to float higher to speak with him on "equal ground," I stayed below to allow him a sense of power and control. "Have you ever heard of the Valley of Death?"

He frowned at me. "Isn't that in Horror?"

"Yeah," I said. "I was kidnapped and taken there as a kid. The Shadow of the Valley ate me, and it's a literal miracle of Horror's God that I'm still alive."

"But you're a spirit," he said, gesturing to my incorporeal body.

"Currently," I said. "You're from Paranormal, right?"

He frowned at me as if to ask, "How did you know?"

I continued, "You know how some people have magics and curses? I have a curse of sorts that lets me join the spirits when I sleep."

He grunted. "Look who's fancy. Why should I care? Why do you keep bothering me every night?"

"Because I want to make things right. Neil, I know what happened. I know why you dress as the ghost of King Hamlet—crying for vengeance. I know who killed you and why you attacked Richard Quigley."

At the mention of his murder, his eyes went wide with fury. However, it was the mention of the Quigley name that sent him into an angry roar. He flew from his seated position to rush down at me. Somehow, I managed to hold strong and stay put. Maybe it was because his fury wasn't aimed at me as he slipped through me. I turned around to find him at the costume storage, grabbing at necklaces, yanking jackets from hangers, and smashing a mask to the floor.

I let him scream out his tirade until a pile of broken costumes lay at his feet and he grew bored.

I floated beside him and gestured to his new mess. "Do you see what your anger has turned you into? Before you were unjustly killed, you were a decent man, weren't you?" I asked. "I sense there's still a piece of him in there. Why else would you turn the lights on for me?

"Then William killed you and got away with it," I said. "Was it jealousy? You had the lead role of Prince Hamlet with Barbara as Ophelia. He wanted your role, and he wanted Barbara, right?"

Neil answered me with a tired nod between heaving, breathing, and groaning... except ghosts didn't breathe. Was he weeping? "Barbara and I weren't even dating. I might have dated her if given the chance, but we were only friends, playing our roles. I thought Willy was my friend," Neil sobbed. "He asked to rehearse with us all the time. Since he was on stage crew, we came early and stayed later than everyone else to practice and play around the theater. I thought he was my friend!"

"I'll make the truth known," I said calmly, "that your death wasn't an accident. His name triggers you into a fury. You noticed Wil-the father and son arguing when the father dropped his son's full name. What I don't understand is why you killed Richard. He wasn't your main target. Did you kill the boy simply to make his parents miserable? Did you know he's Barbara's son?"

Neil's crying only paused momentarily to confirm, "They married? Barbara's son... The boy..." Neil's eyes liquified again as he relived his past. With each sentence, he drifted down with depression. "I was elated with the chance to take revenge, but then Willy left. I was too late. I didn't think it through. Willy was gone, and his boy came looking for me. I thought... Willy would come back if his son was hurt. I hadn't meant to kill him. Only... spook him a little. 'Break a leg,' to 'get in the cast,' you know? Like Willy used to say." The poltergeist chuckled through his sobs, as if to hide his cringing.

"Why did the boy have to fall head first? There was nothing but the empty stage beneath the boy. He shouldn't have died."

A new realization struck me. "His death haunts you. It isn't just your own murder that tortures you now. But there's a reason they call them accidents. People don't get into 'purposes.' Neil, you can't change the past—we can't change what happened to Richard. But we can let both of your spirits rest in peace by revealing the truth. Help me prove Richard's cause of death and your own for justice."

"They'll punish me," he wailed. "Even if I deserve it, I never wanted to be the villain. I was the victim for all these years. The murdered has become the murderer."

"You're already dead," I said. "There's nothing the police can do to you. The only thing that can hurt you now is your own consciousness. Save it by confessing."

Neil cried. "I've done horrible things. I don't deserve to be saved. How would I prove anything, anyway?"

I floated over to him and rested my hand on his shoulder. I actually felt him. "Neil, you're a poltergeist. Look at what you did to the costumes. You can influence the physical, meaning your voice can be heard."

He swung his head back and forth. "The living can hear my moans or laughter, but when I speak words, they're lost."

"You get my drift," I said, waving away technicalities. "You can leave messages and influence the living. Everyone deserves a second chance at life, even in death."

He shuddered, then turned tear-stained eyes at me. "Why?"

Swallowing hard, I reminded myself that he was the product of his situation. Good people often went mad in the face of injustice. I wouldn't condone his actions, but he'd been limited as a ghost to create change in the world. He made bad choices, but that didn't make him a bad man.

"One of the reasons I enjoy being a spirit more than an earl is because death is the great equalizer. Everybody dies, and there's no money here. We can shed our social statuses because we need no kings to create laws, no armies to protect our lands, no reason we can't be whoever we truly are. We dress however we want, spend our time however we want, and go wherever we want. By dwelling on the past and remaining where we are, we create dams on our potential, damning ourselves from reaching for more or becoming more. What do you say, Neil? I'll help you feel at peace again, and you can help me become an investigator to help more people—spiritual and living."

Fresh tears glistened as he looked up to me. "I don't remember the last time I felt peace."

"Then it'll be all the sweeter," I said, smiling. "But you need to be sure about it, because it won't be easy. How about we start by cleaning up this mess?"

Neil's eyes went to the broken costumes. "We?"

I shrugged. "If you put everything in the trash and leave a note for me, then I'll take the trash out and leave the theater compensation to make new costumes."

Neil nodded, then slowly began picking up each broken piece of jewelry and headwear.

The strangeness of the scene was not lost on me. There I was, talking to a poltergeist who nearly choked me on our first meeting…and we chatted about clearing his name while cleaning broken stage props.

People said that life was weird. Death was weirder.

The silence was a little too awkward for my liking. I didn't want to stand there, watching like a warden, so I sat on the floor to remove the illusion of death.

"Thanks," I said. "Now that we're talking, is there anything else I should know about you? Any other people you need to exact your vengeance on or anyone you'd like me to send your last regards?"

Neil swung his head side to side again, placing a fake and plucked flower in the trash. "If I once had family and friends, I've forgotten them in my anger. I expect they've forgotten about me, too."

"Or passed on," I said hopefully. "Maybe once you leave this theater, you can learn if their spirits have lingered. But before you do, I'll need your help to prove what happened to you and Willy's boy. See, I'm trying to become a private investigator of Mystery. In the spirit of complete honesty, I need to solve the mur-eh, boy's Case before the end of tomorrow to be hired in the best agency in Noir."

Neil sat back and frowned. "So, you're using me to get a job you don't even need?"

"I'm asking you," I clarified, "to help me earn a position among the living that will give me access and authority to serve justice among the living and spirits."

He raised a dubious eyebrow.

I raised my hands in surrender. "Why do you think I want to become a private investigator so badly? Other than the fact that I enjoy the work, I need to serve justice to the living and spirits, because if I don't, you guys haunt me until I do."

Neil nodded. "I wasn't always angry. It was the thought of Willy murdering me and getting away with it—getting the lead role and getting the girl—that drove me mad. I didn't even care all that much for the role or girl, but I didn't deserve to die. Then he killed me and got everything he wanted. I hate him." He finished with gritted teeth and a clenched fist that cracked the mask in his hand. The sound alerted him of his anger, and he relaxed. "I only wanted to be in a play, make some friends, and become someone else for a little bit. I wanted to grow up, travel around the world, and make a difference in it."

I nodded. "Traveling the world is…definitely an experience you can't get anywhere else. Unless you read a lot."

He tilted his head at an unlively angle. "You're from Fantasy, right? And you've been to Horror, but now you're in Mystery?"

"I've also been to Romance and Childrens as a diplomat," I said with my most modest shrug. "Once these Cases are closed and I'm an official investigator, I'll have authority to help spirits with their Cases across the world."

"Sounds nice," Neil almost whispered, setting the last broken piece of a mask in the trash.

I glanced out the window to spot the beginning lights of dawn. "Sunset's coming. Meet at my house at dusk tomorrow. I can introduce you to some of the greatest Heroes of Mystery. You won't regret it."

Neil gave me a funny look that mixed confusion and amusement. "You're still a weird kid."

I snapped him a thumbs up. "Now you're catching on. I'll see you tomorrow!"

With a little wave, I left the theater in high spirits.

I slipped into Margaret Norris's house again, quiet so she wouldn't hear me. I spied on her as she watched over my body again, her translucent hand stroking my physical hand.

"I wish I could feel you," I said.

She jumped, and I snickered at the idea of spooking her after Neil had spooked me. Like we were playing a game of spook-tag.

"Y-you seem pleased, Aeron," she said, gesturing to my body. Indeed, I slept with a smile on my face.

"I am. I'm very pleased," I said, floating to her. "It's all re-solved. I'm helping out a poltergeist of all beings, but… it feels right."

"You solved the Case?"

"Yes," I said, "and Neil's going to help me get the job."

I'd be hired as an investigator in Shigaqua. It was my dream job. Everything was lining up.

Margaret pinched her lips and faced the floor.

"Then, is this goodbye?" She slid her eyes up to mine through her long eyelashes.

I tilted my head, confused. "Do you want to say goodbye?"

"No," she whispered.

"Good," I said, daring to drift slowly closer to her. "Because I don't either. I asked you to help me with future Cases, didn't I?"

She lifted her face, astonished by my words and to find me only a breath away. My success with Neil overflowed into con-fidence with Margaret. I felt on top of the world, and I could think of only one way to go any higher. I wanted to share my success and joy with the beautiful spirit before me. She stared at me with wonderment, and I hoped to revive her smile.

"Or would you rather go on a Fantasy Adventure with me?" I whispered.

"I already am," she said. "Once Upon a Time began the moment you parked on my driveway."

"This isn't an Adventure. It's a Romance," I said, then lowered my lips to hers.

Kissing wasn't a foreign concept to me (as Margaret pointed out the other night). I wasn't ignorant of feather-light grazes or passionate embraces. I knew the feeling of a mouth against mine and the other feelings that often rose in my gut.

Usually, when a spirit touched me, I felt a memory of how it was to be touched in that way.

Kissing Margaret was different. I felt nothing.

I opened my eyes to make sure she hadn't backed away. She hadn't, though she hadn't exactly kissed me back with her incorporeal being. She stared at me, wide eyed. If blood still ran through her veins, I sensed that her face would have blushed red.

I leaned back, my high crashing down with disappointment and embarrassment. Unsure what to say, I let her break the awkward silence.

"You kissed me?"

"Tried to," I muttered. I was unable to hug my spiritual friends. Why had I thought I could kiss one? Fool. I hadn't been thinking.

"As spirits?" She laughed nervously. "We cannot touch. Yet you kissed me."

I released an unnecessary sigh. "I might be falling for you, Margaret. You're a sweet woman who deserved more with life. I wanted to offer that to you, but…"

"You love me?" she asked. "Oh, Aeron! I love you too! Does this make us boyfriend and girlfriend?"

A small panic rose in my chest at her exclamation. I'd said I "might be falling" for her, hadn't I? I liked her a great deal, but…love?

What could I say? The words were already out there, and taking them back would only cause confusion. I didn't want to burn the bridge before it was even built. She smiled so wide and innocently that the thought of dampening her spirits (physically and emotionally) made me feel like a monster.

"Margaret, hold on—"

"If you wish me to." Her eyes twinkled with a tease as she reached to hold my hand. My mind accessed the memory of someone holding my hand… The last hand I held was Nita's. Curses, how far down did this spiral go?

Something on my face must have registered to Margaret as her smile faltered.

"Is something wrong? Is it because you are still alive? 'Tis no matter to me, I will wait for you. I may link myself to you and follow you wherever you go. I will be there for you whenever you need me, as long as you refrain from more questionable outings with other women."

"Margaret," I said, stepping away from her touch. "You're beautiful and caring, but I need you to slow down. I've never courted a spirit before, and I'm still trying to wrap my head around how we'd even make it work."

"Simple," she said. "We may go to the beach to talk or to a field of flowers where you pretend to pick one and hand it to me, then—" A ghostly flower appeared in her hair, and she smiled innocently at me.

Curses, she was even more beautiful with the flower tucking her hair back. I forced myself to turn aside and think straight. Phrasing my words in a way to hopefully help her understand, I said, "We can't exchange any real gifts. I can't actually kiss you or hold you. I can't introduce you to my parents. Is that truly what you want in a relationship?"

"I understand your hesitation. Yet we would have every night together, and time is such a little thing. It goes faster than you think."

"Margaret, it's not the time that scares me, it's everything else. I have my whole life ahead of me. I can't spend it all waiting to die so we can officially be together. I can't give up living."

Her smile faded. "In short then, you refuse to commit or be loyal to a single person?"

"You know that's not true with my past commitments, but—"

"I see," she said, eyes casting downward. "Maybe someday you will commit such loyalties to another, but not to me."

"Margaret," I tried again, "these past few nights have all been a dream to me. A marvelous, exciting, and sometimes terrifying dream, but—look!" I pointed at my sleeping body. "I'm asleep! I won't remember half of this when I wake up, and I won't lie to you by promising to stay faithful when I'm awake. I can't keep promises that I can't remember."

She nodded. "I understand. Thank you for the experiences, though. T'was nice while it lasted."

Curses, she was hot and cold faster than a sword quenched from its forging fires. What was I supposed to say? Part of me wanted to grab her into another kiss that would hopefully be better than the first.

No. That would only muddy the waters more. There was no grabbing, kissing, or touching at all with Margaret. I could only listen to her or watch her. Watching her clench and unclench her fists and jaw, I realized what she was really feeling.

"Margaret," I said. "You don't need to push something away just because it's too good to be true."

Her eyes met mine. "Then you agree? 'Tis too good to be true, which means that it must be false."

"Ehhh." She got me there. Once again, my words got in the way of what I meant, but I wasn't sure how to verbally convey my intentions.

"'Tis understandable," she said, returning her silver eyes to the dusty floor. "I knew t'was too good to last. However, thank you for humoring the idea, if only for a little while."

Her lips turned upward into the saddest of smiles. I felt on the inside how she looked on the outside. Breaking a heart didn't mean that mine was left whole.

CHAPTER 16

It is not unheard of for detectives to befriend criminals,
turning them into useful confidants and advisors in the
pursuit of justice. (wait, did I just do that?)

\-   *Lemuel Gulliver's Travel Guide,*
Vol. 4: Mystery
(with notes by Aeron)

Mixed emotions raked my memories when I woke. I remembered feeling afraid, cautious, then relieved and excited even. All those emotions came as I reflected on the time spent with Neil in the theater house. I'd solved the Case? I remembered talking with Neil and coming to some kind of agreement, but…what agreement? Curses, with a poltergeist? I needed to return to the theater to jog my memory.

Sitting up from the broken couch of the Norris home brought back memories of the second part of the night. Margaret. The elation had turned into desire and romance, then dissatisfaction and frustration, until it settled on the ache of loss. I did something stupid and hurt her feelings. I remembered leaning in for a kiss, but couldn't remember the kiss itself.

I groaned and rubbed my palms against my forehead.

174

Curses, couldn't my life ever be simple? Silly, Aeron. Of course not. Life could never be simple when dealing with death.

I packed away my sleeping gear with more mixed emotions. Happy to have the Case solved in time. Sad to leave Margaret. I was usually the one doing the dumping, as my possible inheritance eventually forced me to take things seriously. Stupid wealth and nobility. Killed all the fun.

At least this time, it was the simple fact that I was alive and Margaret wasn't. I could have bridged that gap by dying, but "suicide" wasn't on my list of life goals. That helped convince me that it was partially my choice to break up.

Whatever helped me sleep at night.

I closed the door to Ms. Norris' house, packed my gear into my car, then made my way over to the theater. I didn't remember exactly what I was supposed to do there. Something…left undone. I remembered Neil picking up the broken pieces of props, but…there was something else I was supposed to do…

Using the key from the security, I stepped into the playhouse. Looking around the workshop, my memory refused to be jogged.

Everything was mostly in order…the broken items in the trash, the table and chairs right-side-up. But what was that piece of paper on the table?

The scribbled note addressed to me: "Remember to remove trash and compensate theater. Is this a 'Honey Do' list? Then imprison Quigley." Neil's handwriting was jagged and large, like a child's. Yes, he had the gift of tangibility, but it seemed his motor skills were on level with a toddler.

I smirked. "Thanks, Neil."

The hallway door swung on its hinges, then slammed shut. I jumped at the sound, then stood still, barely breathing. He didn't attack me again. Was that his way of saying, "You're welcome?"

Testing my theory, I said, "I'll take that as a message of, 'I heard you, and we're good.'"

The door opened and shut again, this time a little softer. One slam: yes; two slams: no?

Curses, I was talking to a poltergeist via a door.

Hoping to ignore the chill in the room, I did my chores of taking out the trash, replacing the waste bag, and writing out a sizable check. Once I signed it, I showed it off to the empty room.

"It's signed to the Regal Theater, so no one else can claim it. They should technically be paying me as a private investigator to solve your Case." The door flew open on its hinges then slammed hard against its frame. "But," I added with emphasis, "because you're helping me, and this place has already been through enough difficulty, we'll call it even."

The door opened and closed softly.

"Alright," I said. Curses, I was negotiating with a demon spirit? Desperate times, I guess. "I'll be back before sunset with some friends. After we prove the Cases closed, you can come to my house to celebrate. I'll leave my address on your Honey Do list. Er, if you're linked to the theater, would that be a problem?"

The door closed slowly, thoughtfully.

"We'll make it work," I interpreted. "We'll bring justice to Mr. Quigley for your murder and finally let your soul rest in peace. Tonight."

The door remained in place, and I figured that was Neil's way of saying he was done.

With the weirdest conversation of my life complete, I packed my things and left. I returned to Margaret's house for my car and cringed as my fragmented memories pieced themselves together. I wanted to apologize, but how?

Another failed relationship. Another woman left brokenhearted because of me. I wished to say the situation was new.

Maybe Truth and Nita were right. Maybe I was doomed to unintentionally hurt every woman. But did that mean I couldn't be friendly to them? What about my lunch appointment? I was supposed to make burgers with Nita and Truth later. Maybe that would help me forget the pain I caused Margaret.

I drove home for my usual morning routine, then dug through the testimonies of Richard's murder. Yes, visiting the dead in my sleep gave me all the answers, but I needed to prove my knowledge in a manner acceptable to a judge and jury. No one had seen Richard fall, but multiple people had heard him argue with his father. I called up the auditory witnesses to set up a meeting. After several more phone calls, my first sting was scheduled.

I wrote my reports, scrambling to get all the right information in the right order. I had expected to write two reports to prove 1. Mr. Quigley's innocence, and 2. the real murderer's identity, motive, means, and opportunity. Unfortunately, both parts were complicated. My reports instead involved William Quigley's proof of guilt against Neil Martin, then Neil Martin's involvement in Richard Quigley's death.

William didn't kill his son, but he was a murderer who deserved to feel as guilty as Neil had for his actions. They both deserved to go to jail, though I suspected Neil had suffered worse than a prison sentence for all these years. I needed to convince Mr. Quigley to confess and measure his guilt. How else would I get the poltergeist to stop breathing down my neck?

After another brush of hot air, I set down my pen with a heavy sigh. "Neil, if that's you, please stop."

More hot air blew on my neck, but this time in little bursts, like he was laughing. "Neil!" I jerked around and waved my hands around as if to slap him. I hit nothing, of course.

"Do you want to be vindicated or not?" I asked. "If you want justice, let me concentrate on this report, because if I mess up even a little, it's all over for you and me!"

My pen rose from my desk and started writing on a fresh notepad. "You look crazy."

Like this? Sitting at my desk, talking to no one and waving my arms around at nothing? Yep, I looked like a crazy person. What else was new?

He added, "No wonder you're single."

"Hey!" I grabbed the notepaper and crumpled it into a ball. "I'll have you know that your neighbor confessed her love for me last night! And I have a date for lunch." Alright, I was using the term "date" loosely there, meaning I had a social appointment, but I didn't need to tell Neil that. There was also no need to mention that Margaret and I broke up before we even started dating.

With the first half of the reports done, I decided to take a break and prepare for my lunch "date." I made a list and stopped by the grocery store on my way to Truth and Nita's apartment.

Though I'd only been there once to drop off Nita after dancing, I managed to find my way again. Besides, it was an unspoken acknowledgement among Mystery investigators that everybody knew where everybody lived. We were professional stalkers after all. Truth didn't even bat an eyelash when I stood outside her door, holding a grocery bag of burgers, buns, and various condiments.

For her day off, Truth wore a long and casual tube dress pulled up to her armpits and a knitted cardigan over one arm, draping loosely over her injured right arm in its sling.

"You're early," Truth said to welcome me into her apartment. "Shoes off, please."

Their apartment was—in a word—arcane. There wasn't a single straight line in any of the furniture or walkways. After removing my black loafers, I made my way to her kitchen by weaving around a wooden rocking chair, an oval coffee table, and a colorful crescent-shaped couch with a knitted covering and pillows. Every design of cloth and yarn was inspired by the full rainbow of colors.

The kitchen was another scene to behold with more than the eyes. The air was smokey with a heavy scent of burnt flowers. Pots and pans hung from the ceiling, herbal plants grew in the window, strange fungi grew in jars on the counter, and various liquids jiggled on a vibrator above her icebox. I set my burger supplies between the fungi and sink.

"Is any of this stuff Nita's?" I asked. "Is she home?"

"She has a few possessions in her room. Mostly weapons and exercise equipment. She went out to the shooting range, but should be back soon." Truth answered my responding smile with a downward stare. "You're playing with fire, Fromm."

"What do you mean?" I asked, then gestured to the frying pan. "I haven't even started on the burgers yet."

"You know that's not what I meant." Truth waved me to get to work. "The front left stove burner is broken, so you'll need to use the back right."

"Thanks," I said. "Your home reminds me a lot of my childhood home. Maybe it's the scents." It definitely wasn't the maximized decorations or lack of stone corridors.

Truth smiled. "I buy imported herbs for cooking and burning incense. It's also the sense of magic—which Nita doesn't have, so you might want to be more careful with your interactions with her."

I slapped three patties in the pan and raised an eyebrow. "What do you mean?" I asked again.

Truth sighed. "Did you hear anything I said in the van during the sting?"

"Something about death complicating my life. What does that have to do with Nita? Besides, right after—as I recall—you prodded Nita into asking me out for drinks."

"Do you want me to regret that?"

"No. But you have to admit that you're sending mixed signals. I'd actually given up any romantic interests, but then you pushed her back into my periphery. And, notice, this burger experimentation is not a date."

"Is that what you keep telling yourself? You don't need to keep choosing the hardest path before you."

Did she always speak in riddles? Before I could ask, the front door squeaked open, announcing Nita's arrival. A thud of a heavy bag and metal clinking together echoed from the doorway. When she walked into view I turned around, frying pan with sizzling patties in hand, towel over my shoulder, and grin on my face. "'ello, dah-ling."

Nita wore casual clothes including tan high-waisted trousers, a purple button-up, and a brown leather jacket. Despite the simplicity, she still turned my head as if she walked down a runway. She stared at me with wide and currently green eyes. They went nicely with her reddening cheeks.

Truth slipped her palm down her face.

"Alright," I said, turning back to the stove, "first question for Nita getting to know herself; how do you like your eggs?"

"Well, cooked?"

I laughed. "That's not very specific, but it eliminates raw cookie dough. You know there are more than twenty-five different ways to cook an egg? I usually have mine soft-boiled, but Ruezdad's chef is a master with eggs. My favorite are his omelets. He adds cheeses, peppers, and mushrooms with just the right amount of seasoning." I kissed my fingertips for the sign of perfection.

"Sounds like a lot of work," Truth said.

Nita agreed. "Sounds like a lot of time."

"Worth it," I said, checking the meat color. Not ready yet, so I poured myself a glass of water.

"Is it?" Truth asked. "It's different when you're the one doing the work."

Nita nodded. "I usually make mine scrambled in the microwave."

I choked on my drink, then sputtered, "The microwave? Please tell me you're joking."

She pinched her lips, like she wasn't sure whether to be proud or embarrassed. "It's fast and easy."

"That's offensive to the unborn bird. If you ever come to Ruezdad, I'll have Chef Steve spoil you right. You'll never be satisfied with another microwaved egg after you taste his eggs."

"That's a reason for me to never go to Ruezdad then," Nita said. "I don't care what my food tastes like as long as it's fast and nutritious."

I gagged. "You sound like a trench officer. Are you sure that you didn't serve in the military?"

Truth shook her head. "She doesn't have a military record, which would be regulated and widely available. It's much more likely that she learned her combat skills from a private organization."

I nodded. "Confirming our discussion that she's from Special Operatives, Thriller. Let's move on to the main event. What do you like on your burgers?"

While I offered the usual fillings, Truth contributed a couple of extra toppings from her herbs and fungi. I couldn't remember the name of it, but her red-spotted mushroom was particularly tasty. Nita took a bite from her burger before adding or removing various fillings, eventually discovering that she liked a thin layer of ketchup and mayonnaise, but no mustard. She liked pickles, cheese, and tomatoes, and preferred potato chips instead of fries on her burger.

"Well," Nita said, finishing her last bite of her second burger. "I think that's enough about me. What about you?"

"What about me?" I asked, a little nervous to have the tables turned. Would she ask about my royal family again?

To my surprise, Truth jumped in. "Why do you want to work for Head Investigator Baldi?"

"Why wouldn't I?" I asked. "Silent Sleuth Services is the best agency in Noir. Plus, they're open to hiring Fantastics." I gestured to Truth with a wink as my Exhibit A.

The older woman analyzed me. "Then it's the firm that interests you, not Mr. Baldi, specifically? And you want to work on the Sponsor Case?"

I narrowed my eyes on Nita. "Did you tell her everything we discussed from our outing?"

Nita shook her head. "No. Truth simply knows things."

"I don't know enough to satisfy my curiosity," Truth said. "You were born into wealth, power, and influence in Fantasy, but you chose Noir of all places—where Fantastics and people of color are mistreated? Why did you apply to the SSS specifically?"

I frowned. "Just because I graduated from university doesn't mean I've finished learning. SSS is the most reputable agency in Shigaqua, and Shigaqua's the best place to earn my official license. You work there too. Are you saying it's not the best?"

She squinted a smile at me as if she was pleased, but suspicious of my answer. "Then what do you plan to do when you finish learning? Return to Fantasy?"

"Maybe, someday," I said with a shrug. "I want to start my own investigating business, be my own boss, have my own team, serve justice without worrying about a payroll."

Truth raised her eyebrows. "Are you now worrying more about a payroll than about serving justice?"

I scoffed. "Horror no. I'm serving justice to the Quigleys even though it means losing them as clients and possibly forfeiting my job application."

Nita took a turn to twitch her eyebrows upward. "Mr. Quigley's guilty?"

"Not of murdering his son," I said, "but he's likely to ask for a refund after my report."

Truth, oddly enough, laughed. "I knew there was something crooked about him, just couldn't pin my finger on it. But if that's your opinion, you might want to reconsider working under Mr. Baldi."

I frowned. "Why do you say that?"

She shrugged. "If I knew, I'd tell you. All I know is he's hiding skeletons that aren't his own. Then again, most people have some dark secret that they hope never comes to light."

I gave her a teasing smirk. "Even you?"

She lowered her eyes with a sad memory. "The dark secrets I keep are from the palms I read, but…trust me, you don't want to know."

I opened my mouth to challenge her, but she continued, "I wish I didn't know, so now I'm telling you; you don't want to know. Some palms are better left unexplained."

CHAPTER 17

The detectives, with a penchant for dramatics, take delight in their "stings," wherein they orchestrate a grand unveiling of their acquired knowledge to cajole confessions from the malefactors. (As long as it works...)

- *Lemuel Gulliver's Travel Guide,*
Vol. 4: Mystery
(with notes by Aeron)

I went over the plan a hundred times in my head as I drove to the Regal Theater. Detective Ross arrived soon after I did. "What's this about a sting?"

"You'll see," I said, leading him to the back workshop. "Your part in this will be simple. Just observe and arrest the bad guys when they confess."

He folded his arms and raised an eyebrow at me, but the back door opened before he could ask more. Mrs. Quigley entered, followed by the three auditory witnesses: Mose, Cathleen, and Bernard. Mose was the youngest at fourteen and gave the overall appearance of a sepia photograph with his light brown hair, golden eyes, and tanned complexion. Cathleen was the oldest, having recently graduated from high school. She had lovely turquoise eyes and could easily go into the modeling business with her cropped blonde hair. Bernard was slightly on the heavy side, with dark brown eyes and matching hair with a bowl cut.

Accompanied by two prison guards, Mr. Quigley arrived last, eyeing the theater and other occupants with open curiosity. Mrs. Quigley ran to his side, taking him by the arm, but his guards kept her from further public displays of affection.

I rubbed my hands together like I'd waited my whole life to say my next few words; "I'm sure you're all wondering why I've gathered you here today."

Mrs. Quigley rested a gentle hand on her husband's arm. "We're here to prove my husband innocent, right?"

I clarified, "We're here to do a reenactment. It's actually rather fitting that we'll act out the scene in a playhouse. For the sake of everyone's safety, I need you all to please refer to this man—" I gestured at Mr. Quigley "as 'the father' and his son as such. Do not say their last name." That earned me a few odd looks, but I stared them all in the eyes until they agreed. "Alright, Mose, Cathleen, and Bernard. You were in the workshop, right?"

They each gave the affirmative.

"Where were you exactly when the father and son came in with their argument?"

Cathleen pointed at an area farther into the workshop. "We were working on our costumes, then hid behind a backing flat that was here."

"Let's set the scene, shall we?" I asked. As they cleared the workshop and set up a false wall where they indicated their hiding place, I went back to the security room to ensure the theater cameras were rolling and taping. Returning to the group, I clicked on my personal sound recorder for back up.

Gesturing to Mr. Quigley, I said, "Sir, please stand at the back doorway as you had when you dropped off your son that night. We need a stand-in for the son. Ross, would you mind?"

Ross shrugged and joined Mr. Quigley at the door.

"Fantastic. Everyone else who wasn't present, please step back. Now, the police accused the father of murdering his son. If we may, let's play through the scene as the police described it."

Mr. Quigley scowled. "How will this prove my innocence?"

"Just act like a murderous version of yourself, and the truth should be revealed."

"You don't need to give me acting tips."

"Then this should be easy. Let's go scene by scene. The father and son enter, arguing." I gestured at Ross and Mr. Quigley to play their parts. Mr. Quigley jumped right into his role.

"Why do you despise the theater? Do you think you're better than the theatrical arts? Better than me? It can do so much good for you if you swallowed your pride for even a minute."

"Umm," Ross slurred, glancing for someone to give him lines. "No."

"Come on, Ross. You can do better than that," I urged.

"I don't want to," he added, monotonous. Was that his next impromptu line or his answer to me?

"We'll work on it," I said, then turned to the three young thespians. "You three hear the argument and do what?"

"Feel awkward," Bernard said.

"Yeah," Mose said and pointed at Ross. "His acting sucks."

Cathleen rolled her eyes at Mose and explained, "It was like being caught eavesdropping, even though they were the ones to drop in on us. We, like, looked at each other, then huddled together behind the backing flat."

"Do that," I said. "And you two—" I pointed back at Ross and Quigley "—keep arguing. It gets heated. As the police describe it, the son goes toward the catwalk—maybe to get away from his father?"

Fully engaged in his role, Mr. Quigley shouted, "Don't you walk away from me!" while Ross turned and walked stiffly to the catwalk.

"Please note," I said to the room, "there's no lure for the son to go up the catwalk. According to the police, he had no real reason to go up there in the first place. Go on up, both of you, but remember—for their safety—nobody say their names."

I earned a second round of curious looks, but Quigley followed Ross up the catwalk.

"Alright. As the police report states, the son tore off a button from the father's coat, then the father pushed his son off of the catwalk. Ross, please, take a seat and scream."

"Aaah."

"Come on, Ross. You're a sixteen-year-old boy falling to his death. Scream it like you mean it!"

"Aaaah!"

"Did you hear that?" I called back to the three auditory witnesses.

"Kind of."

"Alright, then here's the important part. The father makes his escape while the three auditory witnesses rush to the scene of the crime. Lights, camera, action!"

Mr. Quigley ran for the opposite end of the catwalk as Mose, Cathleen, and Bernard dashed to the stage. The three youth stopped underneath Ross as Mr. Quigley ran for the back door. His two guards intercepted him before he could make a break for it.

I may have enjoyed myself a little too much as I shouted, "Cut! Everyone, back to the workshop."

With everyone gathered in the workshop again, I addressed the three youth and asked, "You heard the father and son arguing, but you didn't hear the father leaving through the screechy back door? Maybe because you were distracted by another sound, but we'll get to that in a bit. First, answer me this; did you hear him running down the stairs just now?"

"Yeah," they each answered.

I paced between the stage doorway and the catwalk. "So, with your mind on alert after hearing the scream, but before the trauma of entering the scene and seeing the body, you heard the father's escape just now. Would you swear in a court of law and in front of a jury that you heard him running down the stairs during the night of the murder?"

Each of them shuffled or fidgeted uneasily. Mose spoke, "I don't remember hearing anyone coming down the stairs."

I gave a pointed look to Ross. "Let that be added to their statements."

Mr. Quigley, to my great pleasure, had enveloped his role and offered, "Can we try a second take? What if I try sneaking?"

"This is your Case." I shrugged. "But it's an excellent suggestion. Let's try it again, this time, the murderer will be less rushed and more sneaky. Everybody, back to your places!"

We ran through the scene again. This time Mr. Quigley attempted to sneak across and down the catwalk. The three auditory witnesses entered and spotted the man before he could leave the stage.

"See here, everyone?" I pointed at Mr. Quigley at the bottom of the stairs and the three youths at the doorway. "He was caught. Whether he fled the scene of the crime with speed or stealth, he would have been noticed or caught in his attempt to escape."

"Are you saying we're lying about what we heard or saw?" Cathleen asked.

"No," I said, gesturing for Ross to come down from the catwalk. "I'm saying there's no way that this man could have killed his son."

It was enough to cause probable doubt and clear Mr. Quigley of his son's murder. Unfortunately, I wasn't done. Making sure everyone was safely on the ground and gathered on the stage, I paced between the door to the workshop and the empty orchestra pit.

"No, if this man were to kill anyone, it wouldn't be a quick and thoughtless moment of passion. He'd plan in advance, studying his mark's habits and practicing ahead of time. He wouldn't push him off of a catwalk. Isn't that right, Willy Quigley?"

Mr. Quigley's face blanched as I dropped Neil's nickname for him, and a whispered scream echoed through the auditorium. The young thespians whimpered and covered their ears as the adults searched for the source of Neil's scream.

"Ladies and gentlemen." I raised my arm high. "Let me introduce you to the real cause for Richard's death: the Regal Ghost."

Mrs. Quigley screamed as one of the guards became frantic. "What's that sound? Make it stop!"

"Calm down, everyone," I said, then added to Neil, "that includes you. I promised you justice, so let me deliver it."

Once Neil's scream faded and we managed to quiet Mrs. Quigley, I continued, "Cathleen, Mose, and Bernard. You three were the auditory witnesses of the argument between Richard and his father. I want you to think back and remember. Do any of you remember laughter after the argument? Neil, could you give us a sample?"

Neil's creepy laughter bounced across the stage. While most of my audience shuddered and clapped their hands to their ears, Catherine went pale and nodded with little quivers. "I remember. I remember hearing this laugh soon before Richard fell!"

"I...I do too," Mose said.

Bernard squeezed his eyes shut and hands over his ears. "Make it stop!"

"Let that be added to their statements," I said. "It's because of this laugh that you didn't hear the father leaving the workshop. It's this laugh that made the father leave and lured the son up onto the catwalk with curiosity. You've all wondered how Richard had been pushed, how the security cameras went blank at that exact moment, and how anyone could have escaped the scene of the crime unnoticed. The answer is simple: he was pushed by a poltergeist."

"Polar-what?" Bernard asked.

"Poltergeist. Also known as a 'pounding ghost.' They're troubled and troublesome spirits who haunt people or specific locations. They have a special gift for interacting with the physical realm, knocking on doors, moving objects, sometimes biting, tripping, or pushing people such as your son."

Mr. Quigley sputtered, "What's my son got to do with a polar-gust? Ain't that something from Horror?"

"Yes, they can come from Horror or Paranormal states, like Neil Martin did. Detective Ross, please take note of Mr. Quigley's face. Of course, now that I've pointed it out, he's attempting to cover the fact that he recognizes Neil Martin by name, but he's a B-listed actor after all."

"How dare you—Who pushed me?" Mr. Quigley spun around like a spooked cat. "Someone touched me! Who's there?"

"Neil!" I shouted, like commanding a dog to sit.

At the same time, Mrs. Quigley whimpered, "Neil? Neil Martin? Our friend? But his death was an accident."

"Yes," Mr. Quigley affirmed, "his death was an accident."

"Was it?" I asked. "Because your question remains; what does Richard have to do with a poltergeist? The Regal Ghost was previously known for fritzing the cameras and harmlessly moving objects. Why would he suddenly push a boy to his death? This answer is also simple: revenge. Neil hoped to take it out on his killer, seeking justice for his falsely declared death. Except his murderer had already left, leaving his son to fall for his trap."

Mrs. Quigley's eyebrows constricted before she faced her husband. "Bill, what's he talking about?"

William frowned. "Nothing. It doesn't concern you."

I mentally guffawed at his outrageous lie, but managed to keep composure. "Tell me, Barbara, how did you and Willy know Neil?"

"We were friends," she said, her wide eyes still trying to make sense of my words and her husband's clenched jaw. "We met here, during the play, *Hamlet*. I was Ophelia, and Bill started as stage crew, then took Neil's place after…" Her voice drifted as her face slipped into confusion toward her husband.

I picked up her explanation. "Yes, Willy was on stage crew, hanging out with the two lead roles. Let me guess; Willy helped Neil with his lines and stage directions? He led him into position with the spotlight."

"Yes," she whispered.

Mr. Quigley growled. "Barbara, don't say anything. He proved that I couldn't have killed our son. I'm innocent."

She continued to whisper to herself, "I knew you were jealous of Neil even though we hadn't dated. I knew you wanted his role, and you never liked speaking about him after…"

"He didn't deserve you," Mr. Quigley growled. "He didn't deserve the lead role for Hamlet. He messed up all his lines and wouldn't move correctly."

"I thought you didn't like speaking of him because you missed him," she said, her mouth quivering and eyes glistening. "I thought you kept the picture up to honor him. You killed Neil?"

Picture? Ah, right, the picture of their cast and crew with the director holding a framed photo of Neil. With Neil's spirit dressed as the Ghost of King Hamlet, I hadn't made the connection.

"It…it was an accident."

"Bill?" Mrs. Quigley gasped.

I shook my head. "Accidents aren't premeditated, but you knew what you were doing with those spotlights. The video evidence shows you testing your theory that you could lead Neil with the spotlight. But simply leading him off the stage wasn't enough for you. The video shows the pit cleared of chairs and music stands. Every time I came to visit, the pit was empty. But Neil was impaled by the music stands. You staged it for his fall. You led him into the pit with sharp edges waiting for him."

"That was years ago! He didn't deserve the role—he didn't deserve Barbara!"

"Bill!" Mrs. Quigley exclaimed. "I thought they'd forgotten to put away the music stands. Did you set them up again for Neil's fall?"

Mr. Quigley burst, "I did it for you! I did it for us! Getting that lead role jumped-started my career. I wouldn't be the man I am today if I hadn't."

I let his confession dangle in the silence like a hanged man. When the rope settled, I muttered, "The man you are today is a murderer. When you killed a born citizen from Paranormal, his fury and injustice turned him into a poltergeist. He's actually tame until someone says your last name, which you did when Richard ripped off your jacket button. You shouted Richard's full name, alerting Neil to your presence. You left, so Neil did the next best thing for revenge; take it out on your son. Detective Ross, you know what to do."

Ross went to slap cuffs around Mr. Quigley as his guards pulled his arms behind his back. Mrs. Quigley fell to her knees, crying while the three auditory witnesses gaped silently.

Addressing everyone, I said, "Thank you for your cooperation and participation. Mr. Quigley, you have the right to remain silent. The recording of this conversation can and will be used against you in court. You have a right to an attorney, but…they were the one to hire me in the first place. Here's a tip for you. Next time you push your lawyer to hire an investigator, be sure you're actually innocent."

Mr. Quigley choked on his emotions as the prison guards escorted him outside. His grief wasn't for his own guilt. It was for justice finally catching up to him through the death of his son. That was a problem with solving cold Cases. With recent Cases, the crime was fresh in the wrong-doer's mind, guilt still clawing at their souls. But after years of burying the guilt, villains often convinced themselves that they were in the right and felt no remorse.

I left the theater, but not the area, as I had one more piece of unfinished business. Stopping by a flower shop, I bought their biggest bouquet of blue and white flowers with a vase. I walked back to Margaret Norris's house and placed them on her porch, weighing down an opened letter.

> Dearest Margaret,
> Please accept these flowers as a small token of my sincerest apologies. With your permission, I plan

to purchase this lot. I'd like to consult with you on its new construction and renovations. Though we may not enjoy a Romance together, I don't want this to be goodbye.
Until another night,
Aeron

I drove home again to finish writing my reports on Neil and Mr. Quigley. I solved the Case within the week. Barely. I hadn't expected it to be easy, but I hadn't thought it would be so difficult. I leaned back in my chair to stretch my shoulders. Either way, I did it!

I recalled my mom and father telling me stories about the great Jonathaniel Mystery and how terrified and unbelieving he was of the poltergeist they fought. This was my chance to blow Mr. Baldi's mind and earn my place. I didn't just work for the spirits; I fought for and with them. This would show Mr. Baldi that my spiritual visits weren't just for show, they weren't all pieces of cake, but I worked and struggled through Cases just like anybody else. I could work just as hard, and I was up to their mettle.

I went over the reports again to make sure I hadn't missed anything, then prepared for bed. Ahh, my own bed. My favorite hello and hardest goodbye. I looked forward to some good REM sleep after this last week. I needed to check with the spirits and make sure Neil hadn't abandoned me.

Two hours after laying down to sleep, I drifted from my body.

The great James Watson waited by my footboard, giving Neil a wide berth from the doorway.

Neil had changed from the Hamlet costume to the typical fashion of last generation; a button-up collared shirt with sleeves rolled up to his elbows and tucked into his waist-high trousers with the help of suspenders. Without the ghostly make-up, he appeared as thirty-five years old (his current age if he hadn't died). His rectangular face was clean and shaven, but his mouth curved naturally downward, and his eyes were still framed with haunted circles.

I smiled at him. "Good to see you're still here, despite your link to the theater. Was that justice satisfying?"

"Fromm," Watson said curtly, "might I have a word with you? In private?"

I raised an eyebrow. "There's no such thing as privacy among the dead."

Watson's uncomfortable glance at Neil made his thoughts clear. He simply wanted a conversation that was private from Neil. The poltergeist drifted a little, annoyed, but accepting of his detested role.

I sighed. "Whatever you want to say to me, you can in front of Neil. He's agreed to help me clear this Case and serve justice."

"He's a wild card, caught betwixt the realms of the living and the dead. He's out of place in Noir, wielding powers that defy the natural order and verge on chaos."

"Er, all those things you just said also apply to me," I said with a point. Neil blinked at me in surprise. Yeah, he probably hadn't expected me to stand up for him. I hadn't either. "Did Holmes have anything to say about utilizing a poltergeist?"

Watson grimaced. "He may view it as an asset, but remember, he also sees a rubber nose as an asset. You must consider long-term consequences—"

"Neil," I addressed the poltergeist, "you've agreed to no longer terrorize me or those who don't deserve malice?"

He looked down and frowned. "I want justice…for my murder and others."

"And you will help me to prove a point to Head Investigator Baldi?"

He snarled. "If it puts Willy where he belongs and gets you off my back."

Watson raised a surprised, yet suspicious eyebrow. "I still harbor doubts about him. You've become entangled in a web of trouble, and mark my words, it will only invite more trouble. Particularly concerning Mr. Baldi. Are you absolutely certain you want to work under his guidance?"

I paused. I didn't want to feed my recent doubts, but I wondered, "Is there a reason I shouldn't? His agency has the highest regarded teams in Mystery. They solve Cases every week."

"Have you any curiosity regarding what insights the spirits may offer about his past?"

Did I? He was going to be my boss. I knew the importance of rankings and keeping secrets. My parents kept lots of secrets to protect themselves, our family, and the people. I could only imagine the deep secrets that insulated Mystery's walls.

Nothing was secret from the dead, and I was "dead" for a quarter of my life while I slept. Did it matter what I learned? I'd likely forget it when I woke up.

"What do you know?"

"Nothing good." Watson grimaced again. "Your prospective employer has some unsavory secrets hidden away. I strongly caution against joining his ranks, as you may find yourself tangled in his schemes or worse yet, become one of his victims."

"What do you mean?" I asked.

"What do you recall about his predecessor, the former Head of Investigations, PI Harry?"

"Not much," I said. "He was the one to originally hire Truth Locke, and Margaret Norris said he was one of the closest people to catch Sponsor."

"What of Detective Ted Jensen?"

"Detective TJ?" I clarified. "He was on the team to capture Sponsor's main man earlier this week. He was killed in the shooting when the target escaped."

"It wasn't merely the gunfire that claimed his life." Watson frowned. "Your presumed employer orchestrated a series of… unfortunate events that fateful evening to ensure his death. Baldi was overzealous in his ambition to ascend the ranks, targeting and eliminating Head Investigator Harry on a perilous Case. Due to the inherent dangers of such Cases, no one paused to question the possibility of foul play. Subsequently, Detective Jensen discovered the truth and, as a result, was similarly eliminated. Yet the spirits bear witness to the truth. Head Investigator Harry and Detective Jensen?"

Two spirits floated into the room. One was TJ, the detective I recognized. The other had eyes for all business and gave me a stare down that wasn't to be questioned—even if I was of royal birth and had abilities.

He spoke with a gravelly bass like a coffee grinder. "Truth be told, I was entirely ignorant of Baldi's pull when my mortal journey came to an end. I was neck-deep in my own Case, and knew it was tied to Sponsor. I knew it was risky, but went ahead anyhow, driven for justice. It wasn't until I crossed over into the realm of spirits that I got a ringside seat to Baldi stepping into my shoes, listening in on his hush-hush phone calls, tracking his every move, and it hit me how he'd been involved. Usually, as a departed soul, my influence over the living is non-existent, save for the occasional nudge. I nudged Detective Jensen, but was powerless as Baldi set up his premature exit. Then I caught wind of you and your knack. You're still living and can shine a light on the truth."

TJ nodded and added, "Avenge our deaths and bring justice. Take Baldi down and take away Sponsor's biggest mole."

I stared at the spirits, surprised and horrified. Head Investigator Baldi was supposed to be one of the best detectives. Did he earn everything through subterfuge and injustice? My stomach curdled enough that I felt it as a spirit.

"What do you want me to do? I worked hard to get here. I'm not even a real investigator yet. No one will believe me without proof."

Neil quirked his head at me, speaking and reminding us of his unpleasant presence. "As if that stopped you before? You solve Cases. Bring this bad guy to justice the same way you would with any criminal. Do another sting to get him to confess with a recording or audience—whatever, I don't know what you do, just do it! Unless you want to work for a murdering minion?"

"No," I snapped. "Baldi needs to be brought to justice. I… I just don't know how. I've never confronted a corrupted investigator before, especially one I wanted to hire me. I'm not even an official yet. I have no authority without a Permanent Employee Registration Card."

Neil stared at me blankly. "You confronted me. Can he really be more frightening than I was?"

Point taken. But that didn't make it easy.

"Alright," I said. "TJ. I need you to wake me up with a sentence summary of his misdeeds to help me remember it after I wake."

TJ looked at me, confused. "How am I supposed to do that?"

"Er…" I shifted uncomfortably. I hated this method, but it was the only sure way to remember my dream. "I need you to charge at me while screaming something like, 'Baldi killed me.'"

TJ and Neil gave me a perplexed stare.

"Shoot," Neil swore. "That's the best you can do?"

I shrugged. "What else can I do? Are you offering to take notes for me?"

Watson sniffed. "The gift to manifest a tangible form is a rare and contentious gift." He gave a side glance at Neil. "Those few endowed with the gift are bound by strict orders from Beyond, admonishing against interfering in mortal affairs. Any misapplication of this gift results in the severest condemnation of their very soul."

Neil narrowed his eyes at Watson, catching the jab at his poltergeist influences.

I sighed. "I can't ask anyone to do that for me."

Neil frowned. "I just did that for you at the theater."

"No," I said. "I asked you to scream and laugh—no tangible influences. When you started pushing around your killer, I warned you to stop. Anyway, TJ?"

TJ's face hardened, and he spoke with a deadly serious voice. "My name is Detective Ted Jensen and Head Investigator Baldi arranged for the death of me and Head Investigator Harry." Keeping his eyes on mine, he zeroed in on me. "BALDI MURDERED ME!"

He roared, and I sat up in my bed with a jolt. My heart pumped wildly as it recalled in vivid detail the last words. I grabbed the pen and paper on my nightstand to record my thoughts before I forgot.

Baldi was a corrupt investigator. He arranged the death of a man named T…TJ? Detective TJ? The detective who was shot during the escape of Sponsor's main man. And another detective… I closed my eyes and tried to remember the name. Watson had called him Baldi's predecessor. Head Investigator…Harry!

Despite the successful memory, I groaned as I went back to the main detail. Baldi was a murderer working for Sponsor.

CHAPTER 18

The "heroic" detectives frequently harbor their own shadows and secrets of a somber nature. (Seriously, Lemuel? You had to use the word "shadow?")

- *Lemuel Gulliver's Travel Guide,*
Vol. 4: Mystery
(with notes by Aeron)

Alright, you're caught up. Now you know why I woke in a cold sweat with a vivid memory of a dead man screaming in my face, roaring for justice at the price of everything I'd worked for. I hope you've given yourself breaks to eat and have taken care while reading in your comfortable spot, but stick with me. It's not over yet.

Because now that I was awake and leaving my own comfortable spot, I needed to do something about that memory. I was going to prove to Head Investigator Baldi that I didn't just sleep through school. I did more than visit the spirits. I acted on what I learned from them.

Needing a confidence boost before accusing my desired employer of murder, I swung on my unused trench coat and pulled faces at myself in the mirror.

Popping the collar, I lied, "Yeah, I can do this."

A reflection of little Miss Drew shimmered behind me in the mirror. She smacked her forehead into her palm.

"Hey," I defended, "it's cool, okay?"

A couple of the spirits chuckled around me while others released heavy sighs. So much for the confidence boost.

"Whatever," I muttered, and went outside to my car. Walking with the trench coat open and flapping behind me made me feel like a superhero with a cape. Time to save the world. Or at least the city. Did it need to be via the destruction of my career?

The lights were already on at Silent Sleuth Services, confirming late night/early morning workers. I wasn't the only one who worked through the night.

Curses, I had really hoped to work there. I'd even made friends (maybe?) with Truth and Nita, my would-be co-workers. Arresting the Head of Investigations probably shot my chances of employment. Why did I have to be the one to make things right?

At least my timing worked. His secretary wasn't in yet, but lights seeped between the blinds of Mr. Baldi's office. Either he was a super early riser or he'd pulled an all-nighter. I used the secretary's desk phone to call Ross. He didn't answer. Curses, I missed the voicemail systems of Procedural. The only people awake would be the operators at the police station. I gave them a call, but was unsure if they took my request for backup seriously.

Starting toward the office, I released a deep breath and whispered, "Are you ready, Neil?"

A chill passed through me. It was far from comforting, but it confirmed his presence.

Clicking on my hidden sound recorder, I gave Baldi Head the courtesy of a knock before I opened his door.

He looked almost as tired as I was. With his elbow on his desk and his hand supporting his chin, he glazed over a sprawl of papers. A half-emptied bottle of beer sat on a coaster in the corner. He was in the finishing hours of an all-nighter.

He looked up at me in surprise. "Uhh—Spade!" he said, remembering my name a second late. "I thought your time was up?"

"It's barely Sunday. I finished the Case a day early. You know, to give the lawyers time to review my findings." I dropped my file of reports onto the guest chair with a *smack!* and remained standing.

His wide eyes stared at the seat with the reports out of sight and out of reach. Rather than get up to take them, he leaned back in his chair and straightened his tie. "Ya think you gathered enough evidence to satisfy Quigley's lawyer?"

"Oh, I gathered enough evidence and witnesses to save Mr. Quigley from conviction for his son's death, but he's still going to prison. I also gathered enough evidence to reopen a cold Case where Mr. Quigley murdered someone else."

"You did all that in six days?" he challenged.

"And more," I said. "Have you ever heard of a poltergeist?"

"A what?"

"A poltergeist," I repeated. "Please welcome Neil Martin. He's a spirit who can physically interact with objects." An empty bottle on the desk knocked over to the floor. Mr. Baldi jumped back in his seat with a gasp. "And the living," I added as Baldi jerked his arms away from his armrests. I muttered to the air, "Neil, what did I say about touching things?"

"What was that?" Baldi sputtered. "What kinda devil's work is this?"

"Like I said, he's a poltergeist."

Even as I spoke, a pen lifted from Baldi's desk and wrote on a piece of legal paper. "My name is Neil Martin, from Paranormal." Fueled by anger, Neil had picked up entire chairs with ease, but in the regretful unease of confession, the pen moved with the slow scratchiness of a child still learning to write. "I killed Richard Quigley because William Quigley killed me."

Bordering hysteria, Mr. Baldi asked, "What the devils? You brought the devilry here?"

"Yes," I said, giving up on scolding Neil for flippantly using his gift of tangibility, "to prove that I can handle things not meant for the faint of heart."

He brushed at his arm where Neil had touched him and schooled his frightened expression. "You think this impresses me? Is this how you want to earn your job here? By threatening me with magic tricks?"

I sighed. "It's not magic, it's my ability. I already explained the differences. But it doesn't matter. As much as I want to work at Silent Sleuth Services, I won't work for you. I don't work for dirty investigators."

I gave him a moment to think over my words. Then, he growled at me, "What are you doin' here, Spade? You don't belong in Mystery. You're a freakin' Fantastic, even worse than that Locke woman. Ain't ya satisfied livin' off the taxes of your own state? You gotta come here and mooch off ours, too? What's the real reason you're here?"

I scraped away his racist insults to stay on topic. "At first, it was to become a private investigator. I want to help people with Mystery's overarching authority over the mainland."

"At first?"

"Yes." I grimaced. "Unfortunately, my reason for being here tonight has other purposes. See, I learned tonight that you arranged for two men—two detectives—to be killed. The first, was Head Investigator Harry."

Baldi's eyes widened a little. It wasn't a lot, but it was enough to know I was correct. Curses. I had really hoped to be wrong.

"He investigated Sponsor—your real boss—so you arranged for his untimely death. Then, you took his position. Tell me I'm wrong."

"You can't prove nothin'," he spat.

"Ah, famous words of the guilty." I shrugged. "I don't need proof if I have your confession, but I'm sure if I poked around TJ's Case files, I'd find the evidence that incriminated you. At least he came close enough for you to arrange his death as well."

"Detective TJ? Even if I were guilty of anything, what makes ya think he'd have dirt on me?" he bluffed.

"TJ told me," I said. "I spoke to him this morning in my sleep."

Baldi gave me a sly look, as if to catch a bluff. It was no use. We both knew he was the one lying to himself. His sneaky smile fell into a disappointed snarl. "There's a sayin', 'Dead men tell no tales.' And, kid, I preferred the days when that was actually true." He reached into his drawer to pull out a handgun, then aimed it at me.

"Whoa, hey." I raised my hands. "You don't want to do that. Seriously, I don't remember it, but I did some crazy crap when I died temporarily as a child. Also, I have connections with the afterlife who can make your living-life miserable."

Mr. Baldi lifted an eyebrow. "Guilt's already makin' my life a living nightmare. Listen, you're a good kid, and I don't wanna put a bullet in ya, but you're too young and naïve for this game. Everybody's done somethin' they ain't proud of. If ya start diggin' up everybody's dirty laundry, we'll be left without a police force."

Speaking of the police force, I wondered where my backup was. Were they coming at all? Hoping to stall, I said, "Murder and conspiring against the law isn't just dirty laundry."

"Maybe." He shrugged. "Like I said, I don't wanna plug ya, and I won't need to as long as you stay outta Noir and stay outta my business."

"I won't let you get away with it."

"Is that so? How's that when I'm the one holding the gun? And thanks to the reports from the tunnel shooting, I pieced together your little weakness."

He flipped off the lights. My eyes couldn't adjust fast enough to the darkness. Darkness.

Oh. Curses.

Oh, curses! No!

I ducked to the side (collapsed to the ground) just before Baldi's gun went off.

It's never just a power-outage. Echoes of the past threatened my conscience. Except this wasn't a power-outage. This wasn't the Shadow of the Valley of Death. This was Baldi's office, and he'd waited to shoot at me until the fear could grip me. He was going to kill me. He'd already killed two detectives. How many more would he kill to keep his secrets for Sponsor?

Gritting my teeth, I mentally reviewed my fear sessions with my uncle. I listened for Baldi's footsteps around the room, felt the scratchy carpet beneath my hands and knees, grounding myself. Cringing, I forced myself to move in the direction I thought was the doorway. My escape toward light was in that direction too, encouraging my movements. I considered arming myself with my own gun, but I'd be shooting blind.

The lights flipped back on.

"What the—" Baldi was across the room with his gun still trained near my position. Our eyes, however, were trained on the light switch on the other wall.

Baldi lunged for the second light switch in the room.

Off.

On.

"What's goin' on?" Baldi roared.

"Neil?" I asked the air. He was helping me. He didn't want Baldi to escape, either. The lights flickered off-on-off-on like a broken strobe light. It was enough to keep the darkness at bay. The lights didn't stay off long enough to let the blackness swallow me. I whispered a prayer of "Thanks," then steeled my focus on Baldi at the doorway.

Baldi turned his gun away from me to shoot at the other light switch. Neil responded with a creepy little chuckle. Baldi yelled in frustration, then aimed at the light bulb itself.

Before he could squeeze the trigger, I lunged at him, tackling him to the floor like a sportsman. I reached for his gun, but loosening my grapple, let him shove at me. He smacked the butt of his gun against my arm twice before finding my skull. Dizziness threatened my focus. Blackness edged around my vision despite the bulb's brightness.

Baldi shoved at me, and I lost my grip, tumbling back to the wall.

Maybe I could let him run as long as it meant sparing my life. Where could he go that my spirit friends couldn't follow?

I blinked hard and squinted to focus on his form standing above me, his gun pointed between my eyes. Right, he had no plans of running. He wanted me to run, but I refused.

My vision returned only to show me how trapped I was. He'd shoot me before I could even think of an escape plan.

But Neil had helped me with the lights. Could he help me again? Quickly analyzing the small collection of beer bottles in the trash and Mr. Baldi's posture, I had an insanely desperate idea.

"You think I can let anyone else know about Harry?" he muttered. "Sorry, kid."

"Are you sorry?" I asked. "Maybe not yet. You're so drunk, you probably aren't thinking straight. What stupid idea possessed you to think you'll get away with killing me when they hear a gunshot in your office, see my bleeding body, and you fleeing the scene of the crime? You've lost control of your senses. Isn't that right, Neil?"

His aim wobbled between my eyes as he fingered the trigger. "I ain't got any other options—"

Baldi shuddered violently, and his eyes glazed over.

"Wha—" His eyelids fluttered and mouth slurred like a sleepwalker. "Wha's happenin'?"

"Neil?" I asked. "Are you possessing him?"

His gun slowly rotated around the room. "Wha's happening! Why can' I—make it stop!"

I gaped in horror as the nozzle of the gun turned against its master.

"Neil!" I shouted. "What are you doing?"

Baldi shuddered again, confirming Neil's control.

"Neil! Stop!"

Baldi's eyes rolled back into his head. He spoke with a raspy, mutated mixture of Baldi's and Neil's voices. "Why?" he asked.

"Don't murder him!"

"He deserves it," Baldi/Neil rasped.

"What about you?" I shouted. "If you kill him while possessing his body, you'll die too! I don't know how it works, but my mom said that's one way to destroy poltergeists."

"Why do you care if I die? I deserve it too."

"No," I said, surprising myself as much as him. He was a second degree murderer. But asking him to end himself didn't feel right. "No, you lived a decent life. You might have let your mad need for justice corrupt you, but you came clean with me. You said sorry and helped me bring justice at the theater and here. You don't deserve the bad side of the Unknown Beyond. You deserve a second chance, but killing Baldi cuts those chances. Like William, Baldi deserves a trial that lands him in a lonely prison for a very long time. Death is too simple for them."

Neil did nothing with Baldi's body for a few pounding heartbeats. I got him to think about it, but was it enough?

"Stop and think for a moment," I said. "If you kill him, who will be blamed? There's no one else here. Is that what you want? To frame me for murder?"

A small sneer crept up Baldi's lips.

Curses, did I just give him a plan he hadn't yet considered?

"You wanted justice, right, Neil?" I pressed. "Killing Baldi and putting me in prison isn't justice. Help me do this right, and I'll be sure to proclaim you a hero. Not just in Mystery, but back home, in Paranormal. Everywhere I go, the spirits and living will cheer your name for helping me become the best private investigator ever known. I promise."

Baldi's head tilted to an unnatural angle, then his smirk twitched upward. The gun moved again before I could react.

Bang!

CHAPTER 19

The efficacy of private investigators and detectives is oftentimes magnified when they collaborate, pooling their skills and insights for the common cause. *(And the dead make the best team.)*

\- *Lemuel Gulliver's Travel Guide,*
Vol. 4: Mystery
(with notes by Aeron)

Baldi's body collapsed to the floor.

"Neil!"

My shout was barely audible above Baldi's. He howled, yelled, then screamed as a whirlwind funneled out of his mouth. As soon as the mini tornado escaped, he doubled over to grab his leg. A red spot soaked through his pants across his thigh.

Before he could do anything else, I crawled over to slap his gun out of reach. Then I snatched his hands and yanked them behind his back with his own handcuffs.

Curses, it felt good to slide those around his thick wrists.

"I'm putting you under citizen's arrest," I said. "You have the right to remain silent, so shut up."

With my last word, chaos broke into the building as uniforms flooded into the hallways. There was my backup. Finally.

I shouted to direct them to us. Baldi tried to plead innocence, and there wasn't much to back my story.

I explained, "Search the files of Head Investigator Harry and Detective Ted Jensen. They weren't simply caught in the crossfires. They were targeted. Comparing their research on Sponsor should reveal the link to Baldi."

"Should?" the policewoman asked, skeptical.

I sighed and waved my hand, too tired to explain more. "TJ gave me a message. I recorded my conversation with Baldi before arresting him."

Offering my voice recorder, I pressed play and let them hear Baldi's attempt to kill me. They asked a hundred more questions and told me not to leave town, but eventually let me go home.

Thank the Supernaturals.

I left Baldi's office, but my chest burned at the thought of leaving the building. I wandered down the hallway of briefing rooms, offices, and interrogation rooms. Reaching the end of the hallway, I turned back, but still couldn't convince myself to leave. I released a heavy breath, then stepped inside the large briefing room. The room was lined with filing cabinets and chalk boards against the wall and filled with rows of desks topped with note-taking supplies. The sun shyly poked through the skyline and between the blinds, signaling the start of a new work day.

What were my chances of being hired? Sure, I'd cleared the client's name for the Case presented, but I'd incriminated the same client for another one. Then, there was the whole issue of putting the agency's head investigator behind bars.

Even if I let go of my dream to work in Shigaqua's leading investigations agency, even if other agencies were willing to take a chance on me—despite my Fantastic background—what if Baldi was right about everyone having skeletons in their closets? I couldn't accept a job under shady management.

Was that further proof that I didn't belong in Noir?

With a tired and frustrated sigh, I collapsed into one of the desk chairs. I leaned back and stared at the ceiling for an indeterminable moment, unclasp—clasping, unclasp—clasping my leather bracelet. If this was my last hour in Shigaqua's leading investigations agency, I wanted to make it last. I listened to the howls of sirens through the city. Their flashing lights filled the building and reflected off the ceiling tiles. The sirens eventually pulled away, and I sat up.

"Neil," I croaked into the emptiness of the room. "I don't know if you're still here…but thanks."

A piece of notepaper fluttered off a desk and landed by my feet as if blown by a fan. It read, "You're welcome."

I smirked. "You stayed and waited all this time for a thank you?"

A pencil from another desk raised into the air and scratched softly across a notepad. His writing was slow, like a written confession. I stood and walked to the side of the desk, watching his thoughtful writing until he set down the pencil. "I chose a new link."

I blinked. "But you have justice. You could move on to the Unknown Beyond if you wanted."

Neil scribbled his response marginally faster this time. "Good in life, but bad in death. I don't know my future. I'm not ready."

I stared at the piece of paper, almost too scared to ask, "What's your new link?"

Timid and confessional again, my eyes grew wide with understanding and dread as Neil penned each letter.

"Y…o…u."

Curses, crap, and condemnation. A poltergeist had linked itself to me. My mom was going to kill me.

Before I could break out with a sweat and run for the nearest priest, Neil added, "—need help."

My breath stuttered on a cough that was half a laugh of incredulity. He wanted to help me? "Physically?" I asked. "You already saved me from the bullet. That might earn you some good marks, though you took over his body to do it. Not sure how that figures out. But I'm actually alright physically. Just tired. If you're talking mentally, yeah, I've got issues, but who doesn't?"

I ripped off the full topsheet to let him write on a fresh piece of the notepaper. "Spiritually. You need someone to take notes of your 'dreams.'"

I raised an eyebrow at the air beside me. I didn't know where Neil was, but I supposed he was in front of the pad of papers. "I won't ask anyone to condemn their soul for me."

"I already used my gift for bad. Taking notes for a spoiled kid may be good."

I smirked. He gave a nice offer, but I had to wonder, "What's your angle? Why would you do this for me?"

The pencil teetered up and down to tap on the pad of paper in thought. After an awkward minute, he scribbled out a list.

"Because: you're also a good kid, I'm not ready to move on yet, and scaring people is fun, but helping them feels better."

"It does feel good, doesn't it?" I grinned. "I welcome your help, Neil."

I stuck my hand forward to the air, half surprised when I felt invisible fingers and a palm slip beside mine. With a single pump, I shared a handshake with a poltergeist.

"Who are you talking to?"

I dropped Neil's hand and jumped at the sound of a living voice. Truth stood at the doorway with her head angled so hard that her hoop earrings hung perpendicular to her face. She stared at the space in front of my hand as if she could sense Neil standing there.

"Apparently," she said, straightening and adjusting her arm sling, "I get another day off thanks to you. SSS was due for new management?"

I shrugged.

She laughed once. "I knew he was crooked, but couldn't prove it. A mole for Sponsor, no less. I see why they call you Ace of Spades." She approached me, eying me like a horse appraiser. "I hate secrets, but I'll do my best to stop calling you by your Fantasy titles. Still, I get the feeling you're dissatisfied with your Mystery title too. You'd prefer to be called Investigator Aeron Spade?"

"PI Spade," I said, smiling at the thought despite the sadness of knowing that the title was farther from reach than a week ago.

She nodded thoughtfully. "You're as Cozy as a cat solution, but your first hint that Baldi was dirty should have been his reluctance to hire you. You make anyone with skeletons in their closet uneasy, but you'll likely receive plenty of job offers for taking down a Sponsor mole—especially one who orchestrated the deaths of other detectives."

"You think so?" I asked, hopefully.

She nodded. "With SSS under scrutiny, its reputation will sour. I think the stars are telling me it's time to put together a small agency that specializes in speculative investigations. Nita already agreed to join me as a combat specialist, and—despite your palms pointing to death—you survived the week. We'd be lucky to have you."

"You're serious?" I gaped in disbelief.

"As the dog constellation. Most agencies don't supervise their PERCs, promising PI training, but never delivering. I could give you field training to help you pass the licensing exam. What do you say? Partners?"

She offered her uninjured left hand for a shake.

Partners? It wasn't the big and reputable Silent Sleuth Services, but Truth was right about its future reputation. After Baldi's scandal, many of its clientele and networks would look elsewhere. Based on Truth and Nita's performances with the police department, I made a safe assumption that they had their own established networks.

My spiritual friends had encouraged me to make living connections. Was this the connection I was meant to make?

"You said Nita's joining?" I asked. "I don't know if we'll work well together."

Truth, oddly enough, laughed. "Nita's the main reason I'm asking you to join us. You've noticed how much emotion she tends to show?"

"I think the quantifier you're looking for is 'how *little* emotion she tends to show.'"

"Exactly. Except when you're around. Do you know how hard it is to discover the past of someone who's apathetic about everything? You break her shell. Even if it's to shout at you, it's good for her to express herself."

"You're saying I'm good for her?" I asked, slyly. I could make her regret those words. Why did this conversation suddenly feel like I was asking a parent for permission to date their daughter?

"You're good for her as a friend," Truth emphasized. "Don't get all romantic, or you'll screw up everything for both of you. Your love lines are incompatible."

"Alright, thanks for the warning," I said, pushing down my immediate instinct to challenge her. "I'm less worried about her kissing my face than shooting my back. I appreciate your offer, but I'd want to clear it with Nita first."

Truth smiled and gestured behind me. "Why don't you ask her yourself?"

"Ask me what?"

I turned around to find Nita approaching. Her focus was on Truth as if she came to talk with her and only her, but Truth stepped away, saying, "I'll give you twelve hours to think it over since I'm drawing up the business license tomorrow. Today, I'm going to enjoy my unexpected day off. See you around, Fromm-er, Aeron."

I nodded my thanks, then explained to Nita, "Truth asked me to join your new investigations agency."

"Congratulations," she said without a lick of emotion.

Determined to crack her smile, I nudged her elbow with my own. "You know what that would mean, right? We'd be co-workers."

"Yippee."

I barked with a laugh. "Sarcasm! See? I knew you had a sense of humor. Come on, I could help you discover your identity. Not with dates, just getting-to-know-you experiments. We can test every version of Mystery-filled pastries to see what's your favorite, or see some films to find your favorite genres. You can learn a lot about a person based on the kinds of stories they prefer."

Her stoic outer-most layer twitched just enough to reveal an underlayer of irritation.

My teasing smile dampened. Curses, she really despised me. I couldn't team up with someone who wanted nothing to do with me. "Or maybe I'll tell Truth, 'Thanks, but no thanks,' then leave you alone with an apology."

The briefest of glances revealed a concern in her eyes. She turned away to release a slow and controlled breath, then muttered, "I really... really shouldn't like you."

My ears perked at her oddly worded confession. "'Shouldn't,'" I repeated. "That means you do?"

"If you need me to answer that, then you don't deserve a PI license."

I stood there, trying to wrap my head around her words. She liked me, but something told her not to. What? Why?

"Because I'm secretly royal?"

"No," she said. "It's instinctual. Something—I don't know what—tells me that I should abhor everything about you."

I raised my eyebrows. "Sounds like something from your past. That's what Truth hopes will happen. She hopes that I'll help you to discover your past. Isn't that your hope, too?"

She met my eyes again. "Well, what do you hope for?"

I shrugged. "To make honest friends while making an honest living."

Studying me for a moment longer, Nita jutted her hand forward. "Partners?"

"Naw, we need to be more than partners if we're going to work together." I took her hand with a firm grip. "Friends. You can start by calling me Aeron."

"Aeron," she repeated. "I noticed you wince whenever Truth calls you Fromm or the Haunted. Others call you Spade, Ace of Spades, or Digger in Ross's case."

I shrugged and smirked. "I have a lot of titles. One of them might be able to pull some heavy strings to contact the Special Operations agencies."

"Really?" Her stoic expression cracked as her eyes brightened with hope.

"Of course. I wouldn't joke about something like that."

She pressed her lips to suppress her excitement, then pumped our hands up and down like a deal was made. "Friends."

Now, if you asked me at that moment, "Did things turn out the way you'd hoped?"

Horror, no. I'd just shaken hands with a poltergeist and a woman from Thriller who epitomized the concept of Mystery. But I wasn't concerned about my new partnerships. Yet.

If I knew then what I know now, I might have wisely turned tail and ran. I'd just linked myself to someone far, far more dangerous than Sponsor's wildest dreams. But that was the way of Noir. Lines blurred between friends and foes, mentors and monsters, and victims and villains.

You might think, "This isn't an ending. It's the beginning of a new story." And you'd be right. This was only the start of my Adventure as an inspector for specters.

The End

(for now)

ACKNOWLEDGEMENTS

When first exploring Aeron's stories back in Jan. 2018, I hadn't even finished writing "Don't Dance with Death" (Aeron's introduction story), and was still two years away from publishing "Don't Date the Haunted" (the book that started it all). I initially drafted Aeron's series without any expectations of publishing them. They were just my fun stories to write while procrastinating on my others. His stories were shelved for a couple of years while I worked on "Dreaming Princesses" books 1&2, but this first book came to life again after a specific panel at Life, The Universe, and Everything Symposium, 2023. The panel consisted of me and one other author as we discussed ghost stories in fictional and real theaters. This inspired me to set the Quigley Case in a haunted theater, then focus on the Noir setting, giving me that push to finish the story and plan for publication.

As a sequel series to my Haunted Romance trilogy, I wanted these books to be accessible to new readers (who hadn't read the first trilogy), and my developmental editor, Julie Carpenter, helped as my first Guinea Pig to jump into this without knowing anything about Pansy, Theo, or the world of Novel. I'm extremely grateful that her talents and knowledge of storytelling is as expansive as my genres.

I'm ever grateful for my Alpha Readers, RA Cheatham and Jim Doran, who helped me to clean up other glaring errors. Authors make the best reviewers, and I will happily return the favor (and promote their books. PS. If you enjoy my books, look them up because our tastes are similar).

Among my Alpha Readers, I especially want to thank my husband, Michael. He hates spoilers of even the tiniest details, but he still reads my books after I bounce every twist and concept off of him. Thank you for making sense of my "storm-braining." I'm glad I could write a book that was "more up your alley."

After Alphas came my ever-helpful Betas: Bettilee Hunt, Colleen Dowda, Jenny Roemmich, NaDell Ransom, and Spencer Donaldson. Extra thanks to Kat Elmore for being the first to finish and for your love for my stories in Novel.

Last, but never least, I thank God for inspiring me in ways that are just crazy enough to create new ideas, but sane enough that my ideas are interesting to others too. This story was strongly influenced by my own beliefs that angels live among us.

ABOUT THE AUTHOR

C. Rae D'Arc has been involved in every stage of a book's life. As a writer, editor, retailer, reader, and reviewer, she once worked four part-time jobs simultaneously. Thankfully, one of them actually paid her. She received her Bachelors in English from Brigham Young University, and now lives in the Tri-Cities of Washington with her husband and Aussie dog.

PS. To save you from hiccups, D'Arc only has one syllable.

Learn more about the books by C. Rae D'Arc on
her website: craedarc.com
Facebook: facebook.com/c.rae.darc
Instagram: instagram.com/craedarc

"I see you."

Oops, they caught me. The publisher pulled out an automatic firing weapon and pointed it directly at me.

Curses, this wasn't how it was supposed to happen! All I'd wanted was a little information! Would it turn out alright? Was there a happily ever after? Here I thought I could sneak a peek of the ending without anybody noticing.

"Well, I noticed," the publisher snarled. "But here, we don't reward those who skip to the end of books for spoilers. Now, get back to the page where you left the story behind!"